I0667077

Lock Down Publications
and Ca$h Presents

Murda Was The Case 3
by Elijah R. Freeman

First Edition November 2023

Printed in the United States of America

This is a work of fiction. Names, characters, places, and incidents either are products of the author's imagination or are used fictitiously. Any similarity to actual events or locales or persons, living or dead, is entirely coincidental.

Lock Down Publications
P.O. Box 944
Stockbridge, GA 30281
www.lockdownpublications.com

Like our page on Facebook: Lock Down Publications
www.facebook.com/lockdownpublications.ldp

Stay Connected with Us!

Text LOCKDOWN to 22828 to stay up-to-date with new releases, sneak peaks, contests and more...
Or CLICK HERE to sign up.
Like our page on Facebook:
Lock Down Publications: Facebook
Join Lock Down Publications/The New Era Reading Group
Visit our website:
www.lockdownpublications.com
Follow us on Instagram:
Lock Down Publications: Instagram
Email Us: We want to hear from you!

Prologue

Nae turned into the parking lot of the last place on Earth she new Ken would look for her: a raggedy, rundown motel. The text she'd received from Tez was enough to unhinge her. The cat was out of the bag. Ken was in the know about her affair, which meant that she was anything but safe. She knew what it was. This was the bed that she had made. Nae had always known this day would come eventually. It was inevitable. She and Tez had already made up their minds that they were going to be together. This only sped things up. To say that they were utterly unprepared was an understatement. They needed just a little more time…time that they no longer had.

Choosing a parking space furthest from the main road, she cut the engine, grabbed her purse, exited her vehicle, and made her way inside. It was a cool night; not chill, but the relieving kind of cool after a hot summer day. At the front desk was an older black woman, who she paid for her stay and from whom she received her room key. She thanked her, walked out and headed to her room.

As she approached her door a young white girl was coming out with a cleaning cart. That struck her as odd at this hour, but she was too frantic to care. She walked in, closed the door behind her and locked it. Immediately, she cut all the lights off in the room, went to the window and peeked out. Back and forth, her eyes swept the parking lot in search of anything flaky. Nothing. She closed the blinds, took a deep breath, and exhaled heavily. Her nerves were shot. She had just dropped KJ off somewhere she knew he would be good and cared for until she got her affairs in order. And if she couldn't, if or before she died, then he would still be good.

Not wanting to cut on any lights, she went to the bathroom, hit the light, and opened her purse to retrieve her cell phone to text Tez…the letter.

She had completely forgotten the letter from her stepfather Frank; the one that Ken, her husband, had so oddly kept from her despite his passing. He knew these were more than likely his last words to her. She pulled it out, ripped it open and began to read.

As her eyes scanned the pages, she was surprised to find that her father had been cellmates with Ken's friend, Jerome Dew, who she may know as J-Bo. He was coming home soon after being blessed to receive ten years after being falsely accused of a triple homicide. Yes, God had truly been on his side.

What was more odd to her was that as far as she knew J-Bo had a drug charge. She pulled out her phone and searched his name in the Georgia Department of Corrections website. Apparently, he had already been released because there was little to no information on him. Something about the name seemed oddly familiar, though. Jerome Dew…Dew. It wasn't a common last name, and her brain was letting off all kind of alarms. She went to Google and entered the name, and was surprised when the victims from the case her sister had been a witness for had popped up. There was a Fox 5 Action News video. She clicked on it and what she saw made her jaw drop. She did the math on the time…ten years ago…Diamond.

She let out a blood curdling scream.

CHAPTER 1

There were over one-hundred men present at the mandatory meeting personally called by Ken. A big meeting was inevitable. J-Bo and Flip had recently been released from prison after a decade, so everybody knew it was coming. Last night's events boosted the gathering to top priority. Everybody was dressed casually in only solid or dark colors. A member showed up a few years ago in regular street clothes and a white T-shirt. For that he was fined $10,000 and got beat up for the disrespect.

Asia and her cousin Tiffany were also invited to the meeting by Ken for unknown reasons. Looking at the two women present all of the men wore masks of confusion. They all stood on the bottom range of the spacious, furniture less, dimly lit two-story warehouse in Atlanta. Everyone's attention was focused on the top tier where Ken stood above them. The outside of the building looked like a high-quality recording studio for music artists. There were five high-performance speakers that provided superb vocal clarity. Four were mounted to the wall in each corner, with the other one sitting in the middle of the warehouse on the floor.

Looking down at his congregation, Ken smiled. "Young Boss, Young Boss, 25-2, I'll never cross," Ken started. He then went silent, giving everybody a chance to recite their brotherly greeting before continuing. "Tonight's meeting is going to be a little different from the usual. A lot of things are going to take place tonight; promotions as well as demotions," he said locking eyes with Smoke. Smoke dropped his gaze. "And a lot more," he added, shifting his eyes to Peanut who sat in a wheelchair. He stared at him for about ten seconds before continuing.

"Everybody here familiar with Tez as their chief?" They all nodded. "Everyone familiar with Smoke as their senior?" Again, everybody nodded. Ken frowned, rubbing his tongue against the roof of his mouth as if there was a disgusting taste on his tongue. "Tez is no longer Young Boss!" He wished the situation was reversible. The men all frowned and sent silent stares to each other as if asking, "What the fuck?"

"And he was not respectfully discharged," Ken continued. "He's actually on the run, living in seclusion with..." He took a deep breath and flipped the few loose dreads that had fallen over his face to the back of his head. "With my wife. And both of them... D.O.S!" It was so quiet as his words lingered in the air it sounded as if no one was even breathing. Everybody looked like they'd seen a ghost. Some mouths dropped, some scratched their heads, some eyes grew big as saucers, whereas others were grinning on the sly.

"Smoke," Ken said, causing everyone to divert their attention to him. "Smoke is no longer a senior boss. Even though he was merely following orders from our chief. . . ex chief, everyone know how that goes." He looked at Peanut. "Plus, he almost took the life of a very loyal and respectable brother. Smoke is now a baby boss, and he is in major violation."

Smoke's eyes instantly watered. He dropped his head and wiped his eyes before a single tear could fall. Looking back up he motioned for Snag, whispering in his ear. Snag nodded, and made a hand gesture towards Ken. Ken nodded, and Snag handed Smoke a microphone.

"Young Boss, Young Boss, 25-2, I'll never cross," he greeted softly. "After I found out the real reason Tez wanted shawty dead." He looked at Peanut's fragile body in the wheelchair for a split second then back at Ken. "I felt like shit, bra. I knew I would be in trouble, but I- I- I didn't think I would be stripped of my rank that I worked over ten years for." His voice cracked, and he couldn't control the tears any longer. They flowed freely down his face. Ken looked at Snag firmly. Knowing what that meant already, Snag took the microphone away from Smoke.

"I'm going to say this last thing before I pass the mic," said Ken. "How many of you are familiar with J-Bo?" Half of the room raised their hands. "Well, for those of you who don't know who he is," Ken looked back towards the dark area in which he came from and waved. J-Bo came and stood beside Ken. They shared a long brotherly hug. "J-Bo is my best friend and little brother. Him and his cousin Flip, whom you all will meet when he gets out the hospital, killed three people: a nigga and a pregnant girl for stealing from us. They got jammed up and sent away. I was able to make sure they didn't have to do life in prison." He paused, looking into everyone's eyes. "So, after ten long years in the dungeon, he's finally home. J-Bo is now the M.B.A. .... I love you boss!" He handed J-Bo the mic and took a seat. Everyone clapped.

"Young Boss, Young Boss, 25-2, I'll never cross," he greeted. Everyone repeated. "As y'all know, I'm J-Bo. Everything I'm finna say done already been discussed between me and da big bro." He nodded towards Ken. "But for the most part these are his words. . . Peanut, step up brotha!" Tiffany lifted the lever of his wheelchair lock and pushed him until J-Bo instructed her to stop in the middle of the floor. Peanut flashed a smiled that seemed like it hurt to do.

"Peanut, I'm sorry bout what happened to you lil bra, and we respect ya request. But I got sum betta for you," J-Bo said. Snag handed Peanut a mic. "You are now Young Boss primary chief," J-Bo finished. Everyone smiled, liking the idea of Peanut being their chief. Peanut struggled, slowly raising the mic to his mouth. Seeing his obvious difficulty, Tiffany held the mic for him. Peanut sighed.

"I joined Young Boss almost eleven years ago," he spoke. All the guys started frowning, feeling some type of way about Peanut not using the mandatory respectable greeting. Ken and J-Bo remained calm, knowing exactly why he didn't. "I've met some people that I love to death. And I've done some things that I'm a take to da grave with me on behalf of Young Boss." He looked at Smoke as Smoke looked down. "I really appreciate the opportunity to be chief over this one-of-a-kind, glorious organization." He locked eyes with Ken. "But I want out. I want to live for God."

These niggas finna kill us, Tiffany thought.

Snag came walking swiftly from the side of one of the big speakers, pulled a 9mm from his waist, and place the tip of the barrel on Peanut's forehead. Peanut looked in Snag's eyes. Snag turned his head to J-Bo and Ken, searching both of their eyes for any sign to pull the trigger.

"Peanut, I told you this was a set-up! I told you these heartless-ass-niggas wouldn't spare you," Tiffany cried, looking down at Peanut. One of the older men from the crowed approached, drawing his .357 magnum, and placed his aim on Tiffany.

I knew doing shit the right way wasn't gone fuckin work. These niggas don't give a fuck bout a nigga tryna get himself right wit God. These mothafuckas prolly don't even believe in God, Tiffany thought, as she felt her body trembling and palms sweating. She looked at the older man holding the gun. His head was bald, thick beard neatly lined, and his eyes were empty. He seemed to have no soul.

"Step away from, Peanut," the older man ordered her. She let the mic rest in Peanut's feeble grip and leaned in to kiss his lips, tears flowing freely down her face.

"He gone kill my cousin?" Asia whispered to Smoke. Smoke quickly squeezed her hand and placed his index finger over his lips. Smoke knew any form of side jargon would be looked upon as disrespect, and he didn't want any extra problems. Asia slipped her hand in her purse and clutched her .38 special. She had bought the gun after Smoke beat her ass and drug her out of the club one night.

Peanut looked in J-Bo's eyes. "I just want to live right, big bra, please," he pleaded.   J-Bo turned his mic off and spoke to Ken for a few seconds. He turned the mic back on and spoke.

"Peanut, you know twenty years in is one way to be discharged respectably. You also know you just disrespected every brotha in this room, and around the globe when you didn't spit that greeting!" His voice was hard.

Peanut nodded and looked at Tiffany. "I love you, baby," he whispered. Tiffany started weeping harder. Asia gripped her revolver tighter.

"How many of y'all say Peanut's life should be taken away tonight?" J-Bo asked. Everyone raised their hands except for Asia, Smoke, and Tiffany.

"Snag," J-Bo said

"What's up boss," Snag answered, not taking his eyes off Peanut.

"Put ya gun down."

Snag thought he was hearing shit. He looked up at J-Bo. J-Bo confirmed what he said with a head nod. Snag reluctantly returned the gun to the holster on his hip. Peanut took a deep sigh of relief.

"Ty-Ty, put ya gun down," J-Bo said to the older man with his weapon on Tiffany. Ty-Ty lowered his weapon. Asia then released the grip on her gun.

"Peanut, we really appreciate you for doing what you did," J-Bo said, confusing everybody. "Tez was in a real high position, and da fuck nigga crossed a major line. He betrayed the big bro in a major way, and Peanut brought that shit to light," he said, looking around the crowd. "And for that,

Peanut almost lost his life. ... Peanut, from the Mega boss, and the M B.A." He paused to look at Ken, who nodded. "We grant you a respectable discharge. Go live fa God, bra." He then looked at Tiffany. "Thank you, too. We appreciate you."

Peanut struggled with the mic again, andTiffany held it for him.   "Thank y'all very much," he said. Tiffany took the mic from Peanut, gave it to Snag, and quickly wheeled Peanut out of the warehouse.

"Smoke, yo violation finna happen tonight," J-Bo said, before nodding to Snag.

Snag patted Smoke down. He wasn't strapped. Snag then handed his gun to Ty-Ty, before randomly picking five young niggas to help him out. They formed a straight line, one behind the other. Smoke stepped forward.

BAM!

With all his might, Snag's fist crashed into Smoke's face. They fought, swinging wild and forceful punches for two minutes straight. Ty-Ty, using the stopwatch on his phone, would tell them when the time was up. Once the clock stopped, Ty-Ty would yell "stop" and restart it. Snag would then move out the way and the next man in line would step up. That cycle would continue until everyone had a turn to fight Smoke for two minutes each.

Twelve minutes later, Smoke was a bloody mess. Both of his eyes were swollen shut. The entire front of his dress shirt was saturated with blood. Ty-Ty gripped him by the shoulder and escorted him to the bathroom to get himself cleaned up.

"Asia, step up," said J-Bo.

She walked around the guy that was mopping up blood, and stopped in the center of the floor. She looked around for Smoke, but he hadn't yet returned. Her hands were fidgeting. She felt one of the men nudging her back, causing her to step farther up.

"My people say you got some real good values, and we think you will be a good asset to Young Boss. You can be the first female to ever be put down. And for the loyalty you done showed, we willing to make you a grown boss. That's three ranks under me, and over the ladies. You can be chief. We believe it's time to add some women in this family. We're not a gang, just a respectable group that stands on love and loyalty. Would you like to join as the first respectable sister," he grinned.

Snag came from the back and handed Asia a mic. His hand was wrapped with a white bandana.

"Yes, I would love to join," she answered half-heartedly.

J-Bo smiled, and diverted his attention to the crowd. "I already said this once, and I'm a stress it again. Martez Challey, better known as Tez. . . D.O.S.! And Nae Griffith, I meant, Nae Waters, wateva she goin by, D.O.S.! I wouldn't giva fuck if you seen them in church on they knees, praying to God for forgiveness. You betta walk up behind him or her and put a bullet in they head." J-Bo paused, taking time to look in everyone's eyes. "We got a million dolla reward on Tez and Nae, each. Got me?"

Everyone nodded their understanding.

"When Flip gets out the hospital, we finna throw the biggest party ever. So brothas and sistas," he winked at Asia. "Get ready for the turn up!" Everybody clapped. "Young Boss, Young Boss, 25-2, I'll neva cross," J-Bo said, and everybody reiterated. Smoke was coming from the bathroom when through his blurry vision he saw J-Bo waving for Asia to come up to the top where he and Ken stood.

The top tier is only for niggas with rank. Bitch you not Young Boss. Why the fuck you walkin' up them steps, Smoke thought. Ken hugged Asia and whispered in her ear. "I seen you clutching when you thought Ty-Ty was going to do your cousin. I respect the loyalty, but had the wrong eyes seen you, you would've been dead without my approval, okay?"

"Okay." She whispered back.

CHAPTER 2

The next morning, Ken was in his bedroom sized bathroom undressing. The only thing that occupied the counter top was an electric toothbrush and a gold jar. His thick dreads stopped in the middle of his back. Once undressed he broke the rubber band that held his dreads together, and allowed them to freely flow apart. His face seemed rougher than before. He opened the gold jar and applied a finger full of the revival cream to his face. He rubbed it in. After he was fully undressed, he slowly, lazily, stepped into the walk-in shower.

He turned the knob all the way to the H, allowing the water to grow extremely hot. As he scrubbed his body with Dove soap, the piping hot water seemed to cook his skin. He flinched but did nothing to get out the way. He didn't give a fuck. His heart was in more pain than the hot water could do to his body on any day.

What the fuck could I have done to make my wife go fuck on my young nigga? What the fuck did I honestly do wrong? I gave this bitch the world on a silver platter, Ken thought. It had to be something. She got this big ass house, nice cars, I invested in her career, got this bitch a whole fucking business. Maybe it's the time I was busy and couldn't spend with her. Fuck that shit. No more making excuses for this punk ass bitch.

Stepping from the shower, he dried off and dressed simple; a black pair of vintage blue Robin's jeans, a black T-shirt, and a pair of black and white Yeezy shoes. He looked in the mirror and rubbed at his growing beard, making a mental note to get it knocked back down to a designer stubble. He walked into his son, KJ's, abandoned room. Ken smiled, looking at KJ's bed, toys, and coloring on the walls. He laughed, remembering how his son used to always sit on the bed Indian style as he watched cartoons. He shook his head and wiped at his eyes before tears could form.

Back in his bedroom, he picked up his phone off the bed and dialed for Nae. No answer.

Punk ass bitch took my child away from me, he thought.

He aimlessly fingered through the apps on his phone and then it hit him! . . . . .

Once he saw the *I Got You*app, he remembered how helpful it was finding Nae's whereabouts last time. His fingers began to shake and he quickly clicked on the app. Nae's phone number appeared directly under his with a button beside it that said, *find me*. He clicked on it and an address popped up. The location was thirty minutes away. It said her phone had been at that address for ten hours. He ran to the closet and got his .45 semiautomatic and tucked it. He snatched a black and white wool varsity jacket from a hanger and pulled it over him. He slipped on some Nikes, grabbed his keys and rushed for the door.

***

J-Bo picked Asia up early that morning to teach her the necessary things she would need to become an official ranking member. He took her around all their trap spots throughout Atlanta and made introductions so her face would be familiar.

"Now this last spot we finna go to isn't a trap spot. This a safe house," J-Bo said, his voice deep. He glanced over at Asia, then back at the road. "You hear me," he asked.

She nodded. "Yea, I hear you."

"You know what a safe house is?"

She shook her head.

"So why in the fuck is you saying 'yea, you heard me' if you don't even know what I'm talkin' bout? You betta learn how to ask questions, shawty! Because this shit real out here, and we ain't babies. So ain tryna be tellin' you shit more than once. If you don't know, ask, okay?"

She nodded.

"A safe house is where you go to if you in trouble. If you just need a minute to figure shit out. It's in a good area, so we ain gotta worry about the spot being hot. And they do a whole lotta countin' up here," he said.

They pulled up to a big house in Villa Rica. Getting out of the car, she admired how each house's lawn was mowed perfectly at the same length. The house held three garages for cars. J-Bo dug in his pocket for a single key and opened the door.

"Snag!" He hollered as they entered. "Yo Snag," his deep voice blared through the house.

"Why are the walls blue," Asia asked.

"Blue represents freedom. Niggas can feel free here," J-Bo answered.

This shit definitely big enough to feel free in, Asia thought, looking around the spacious living room. There were two sectionals, two 70 inch flat screens mounted to the wall, and a small table with a pound of broken up weed on it.

"Yoo," Snag answered, coming down the steps, pistol in hand.

"This Asia, grown boss. Asia, this Snag," J-Bo introduced.

"Yea, I remember her from last night. Welcome to the family, sis," Snag said.

"Thank you," she replied, looking in his mouth, realizing why they called him Snag.

"I'ma make this quick because I got shit to do. She's off limits for anyone except Smoke. Got me," J-Bo asked, staring deep into Snag's slanted Chinese looking eyes.

"Yea," Snag answered, quickly shifting his eyes to the floor then back up.

16

"Also, I need fifty thousand for her right quick, and somebody to do personal security."

"Security for you," asked Snag.

"No. For her. Who else here with you?"

"Just me for now."

"Well, I need you for security until I find someone."

"Aiight, let me go grab the money," Snag said, running back up the steps.

***

Ken turned into the parking lot of a raggedy ass, rundown motel. Good thing he decided to drive his Escalade instead of the Ferrari. That would've been way too much attention. The motel was a one story, long double-sided building with twelve rooms on each side. An old man and woman were sitting on the curb. They appeared to be zonked. Ken parked in one of the many available parking spaces and pulled his gun from his waist, resting it on his lap. Two other vehicles besides his occupied the parking lot: an old white station wagon, and an old Impala with no wheels.

Ken looked down to his phone, going through the app. It showed that he was at the right location, but it didn't reveal the room number of course. He waited diligently for something miraculous to happen. The only thing happening was those two drunks on the curb, pointing and laughing at shit that didn't exist.

After thirty minutes of waiting, two maids appeared from different rooms: an older black lady and a young white girl. The older black lady removed some bedspreads from her cart and returned inside the room she was working on. The younger white girl was sending a text or whatever she was doing on her phone. The strong March winds had started cutting. She dropped her phone in her uniform's pouch and started to take some bedding from her cart.

Ken pushed the horn a single time. She looked up. He motioned for her to come. She scurried to his truck, trying to weave the winds. He leaned over to open the passenger side door.

"Hi, my name is-," Ken was saying.

"Oh my gosh, your Kenneth Your artists are on tour right now! I've been keeping up with you guys on my phone. I fucking love you guys," she exclaimed, as she entered the passenger seat.

Ken examined the scarring, widespread acne all over her face, and the blackening teeth.

Bitch is definitely a meth head, he thought.

"Yea, that's me. I'm going to be headed out to meet them soon. I'm just here to handle some business. If you can help me, I'm sure I can hook you up with backstage passes and get you away from this bullshit ass job." He nodded to the building.

"Oh my gosh, really," she squirmed.

Ken nodded and went through his phone until he found a picture of Nae.

"Is she- well, I know she's here. What room," he asked.

She got closer to the phone, locking in on the screen. She nodded in assurance.

"Yea, man. She's here, her and a guy. He slim, dark skin, and…"

"Which room," he cut her off. He knew she was describing Tez.

She stared at him with those dreamy, icy blue eyes. "I will tell you but…"

"What you want, some money?" He dug into his pocket.

She shook her head no, slowly and seductively as she stared at his zipper.

"I want you to fuck me and I swear to God, I'll give you the key to that girl's room."

Ken thought about it for a minute then shook his head. "Look baby, we're not about to be doing this. I'll give you two thousand dollars right now."

She opened the passenger door. "I don't want the money, hun."

Ken grabbed her arm before her foot could touch the ground.

"Okay, okay, close the door," he said reluctantly.

She quickly closed the door, pulled her skirt up, and slid her panties to the side.

"Hold up, listen. I don't feel like doing this shit," he said.

She started to leave again. He grabbed her again.

"I'll let you give me some head," he bargained.

She agreed with shoulder shrugging and a big smile. When he undid his pants and pulled out the short, thick slab of meat, her pussy started throbbing. She frowned when he pulled a condom from the glove compartment and put it on. She started sucking his dick while it was soft. Ken turned his head, looking out the window. As he grew harder she took more of him to the back of her mouth, making more and more spit drop from the back of her throat. Ken used his top lip to press against his nose. *Damn her fucking mouth stink*, he thought. He grabbed a handful of her blonde hair and begin pushing her head into his lap. She gagged loud, but never stopped him. He nutted seconds later. He pulled the spoiled condom off and started to toss it out the window.

"Wait! Please, Ken. I wanna taste it," she said.

He handed it to her and she squeezed all of the thick content inside her mouth. He took it from her and tossed it out the window. He then looked around the truck for something to dry his lap with. She put her head back in his lap.

"Nah, hold up," he pushed her head back.

"I'm not gonna suck your dick again. Just let me clean up the mess."

She licked and slurped his inner thighs, around his dick, and his balls until all the watery saliva was back in her mouth and traveling down her throat. Ken pulled his pants back up and stared at her. She fumbled with some key cards in her pouch.

"This is the master key card. I'll need it back." She handed it to Ken. "Let me see that picture again," she said. He showed her again. "Yep, that's her. They got here last night; room two-eleven. I'll be at my cart when you come out. If the old lady is out here with me just drop the card and keep walking," she instructed. Ken pulled the pistol from under his leg, tucked it, and got out. . .

***

"You gotta license?" J-Bo asked, approaching the truck.

"Yea," Asia retorted. He gave her the keys and went to the passenger side.

"So, I got a question," said J-Bo, propping his feet on the glove compartment. "What you really want?"

She blended into traffic, quickly stopping at a stop sign, looking in his eyes. "What you mean?"

"Out of being Young Boss. Especially rankin'. What you want?" he asked again.

"Shit, I don't know. Learn the operation, I guess."

J-Bo laughed. "Listen, big bra got two M's on two people head." J-Bo shook his head. "That should be everybody's damn goal. Even if you catch one of them mothafuckas and get an M, you'll be good," he explained.

"So was Tez fuckin da shit outta Nae for real?" Asia asked in disbelief.

J-Bo nodded. "Why you gone ask a question to some shit you already know?"

"I don't know for a fact. I mean, I heard people say it."

"Yo cousin the one recorded him fucking her. You mean to tell me she ain't show you that video or at least tell you about it?"

"She didn't. I really haven't even heard from her every since Peanut been talking bout living for God. She just kinda fell back. Like I don't know if she on the same shit or what," Asia explained.

J-Bo nodded. "Yea, he was fucking her. And I want them two M's."

"Where we going?" Asia asked, at a light, not knowing whether to turn or continue straight.

"To the hospital. We gotta go see Flip," J-Bo answered.

***

Ken causally walked across the lot searching for room two-eleven. The outside smelled like piss. Ken used his upper lip to wipe at his nose again. The notion of him going into this room today and killing his wife, as well as his young nigga, is moot. There were no second guesses, feeling bad, or questioning. He was fully prepared to put a bullet in both of their domes. Once he reached the last room, he looked at the sign on the door. It said one-eleven.

Two-eleven has to be on the other side, facing the woods. Even better, Ken thought. He made his way to the other side, having to leap over a muddy area so he wouldn't fuck up his Nike's. His heart skipped a beat when he made it directly in front of room two-eleven.

I wonder if my son is in here? I wonder if Nae's going to have anything to say before I pull the trigger, he thought, pulling the key card from his pocket. He looked around for witnesses. There were none. He pushed the key card into the slot. The light on the lock went from red to green, and he slowly pushed the door open.

Entering the room he took a deep and slow inhale. *I can smell her*, he thought. He quickly and quietly pushed the door closed behind him and pulled out the .45, aiming it in the dark room. He held his position for a few seconds so his eyes could adjust to the darkness. Once adjusted, he could see the room properly. Two beds. There was a small figure on the first one. He rushed to it, knowing it was his son, only to find some crumpled up sheets. On the next bed was Nae's cellphone connected to the wall charger. Tez's cellphone was on the dresser. Ken looked up as he heard talking from a distance. He quickly turned the aim of his gun towards the bathroom, but to his dismay no one came out. The shower water had just turned on. He went through Tez's phone and read a text sent to Nae the other night: DO NOT GO HOME! KEN KNOWS.

Ken used his t-shirt to wipe his finger prints off their phones, and dropped them back on the bed. He approached the bathroom. First there was a faint noise that grew louder the closer he got; moaning and skin smacking together.

"Aww shit, Nae. Dis pussy so mothafuckin good," he exclaimed. "Who pussy is dis, shawty," he asked followed by a loud smacking sound.

"It's yo pussy, T!" Her voice was more high-pitched than he'd ever heard.

"And who else?" he asked, the skin smacking speeding up.

"Nobody else! It's all yours, T," she cried.

"Fuck dat otha nigga. It's me and you now, undastand?"

"Yes daddy! I understand," she yelled, her head bumping into the shower wall.

"I'm cumin Nae!"

Ken kicked the thin door open, training his gun at the naked couple in the shower. It was a young couple, probably twenty years old, both brown skinned.

"What the fuck!" Ken angrily spat.

Both of the young people's hands went up in the air.

"I- I'm sorry bruh! She told me she was single," the young boy said.

What type of trippy shit is this, Ken thought.

"Where did you get them two cellphones from," Ken asked.

"I was checkin' out dis mornin'. Dis nigga and his girl gave me da key. Say dis room paid foe fa da next three nights, and dem phones was in here. But you can take em if you want em."

"Why the hell are y'all calling each other Nae and T," Ken asked suspiciously.

"Her name Renae. My name Lil Terrance."

Ain't no mufuckin' way, Ken thought. He lowered his weapon and laughed. Pulling out his phone, he went to the photo gallery in his phone and found a picture of Nae.

"Yea, dat's her," Lil Terrance said upon seeing the photo.

Ken apologized, dropped two hundred dollars on the sink and left.

Outside, he returned the key card to the white girl and asked her what name the room is in, and was it paid for with a debit or credit card. She went into the small office and returned a few minutes later.

"It was paid in cash. Name on the room is Michael Jordan," she informed.

CHAPTER 3

"What's good, my boi?" J-Bo smiled hard as he and Asia entered Flip's hospital room.

Flip smiled. "What's good, nigga?" He raised one arm, stretching it out to hug J-Bo, who hugged him then looked back to Asia.

"This Asia, grown boss, and chief over the women," J-Bo explained, as he sat on the bed with his cousin.

"Since when there's females in Young Boss, especially ranking?" he frowned.

"Since last night, nigga," J-Bo laughed. "You our new chief."

"What? You a gotdamn lie!" Flip exclaimed.

J-Bo laughed and looked to Asia. She chuckled.

"Am I lying?" J-Bo asked.

She shook her head. "Nope. Flip is chief," Asia answered.

"What happened to Tez?" Flip was baffled.

"D.O.S.," J-Bo mumbled.

"Damn, for what?"

"Got caught fucking Ken's ole lady. But that ain't even the kicker."

Flip raised his eyebrows. "What?"

"Ken put an M a piece on they head. So, I need you to hurry up, heal up, and get outta here, so we can get this money, Cuz."

"An M?" Flip took a deep breath. "We just did a ten."

"Yea, bout two-fifty. This bout two M's," J-Bo reassured. "Anyway, how yo hand?"

Flip raised his arm from under the sheets. His entire left hand was covered with gauze and what looked like a cast of some sort.

"They put my hand back on last night, but say they couldn't reattach the nerves. So, I won't be able to move it again," he said reluctantly.

"I'm just glad you alive, nigga," J-Bo said, looking at Flip's hand.

Asia's phone rung. "It's Smoke. Can I step out and talk?" She asked.

"Yea, go head," J-Bo said.

"She strip at D.O.A.?" Flip asked the second she stepped out the room. Diamonds Of Atlanta is an adult entertainment nightclub.

"Yea, but shiiid, she Young Boss now, and she off limits to anybody but Smoke."

"Why him?" Flip asked, scratching his nappy afro.

"Because they been together," J-Bo answered.

"That's wassup." Flip smiled. "He made you da M.B.A. Damn, so yo word just as good as Ken's now, huh?"

"Hell yea, nigga. And big bra really tryna focus on the music shit so..." J-Bo rubbed his hands together. They both laughed.

"So, what's next?" Flip asked.

"Ion know about y'all, but, I'm finna find this nigga Tez and get this M."

"If it was that easy a nigga woulda been found em," Flip said.

"Nah, nigga. The shit just happened, like recently type shit. Ain't nobody been lookin yet. But I need you to rest up and get better so we can celebrate."

J-Bo gave Flip a quick update of the events that had transpired since they'd been released.

"Okay, okay. So y'all just let Peanut dip?"

"Yea, man. Wasn't nobody expecting that. Snag wanted to pop him." J-Bo laughed hard, remembering Snag's facial expression when he told him to put his gun down.

"Shiiid, I bet he did. A nigga ain't neva left Young Boss like that, at least not alive."

J-Bo stood up and stretched. "Who brought you that?" J-Bo nodded to the iPhone in Flip's bed.

"Daneisha," Flip mumbled.

"Cuz, I know she held it down for you, but…" he stared in Flip's eyes.

Asia walked back in the room.

"Ain tryna hear dat shit, J-Bo." Flip looked out towards the window.

J-Bo sighed. "All I'm sayin is…"

"I don't wanna hear that shit, J-Bo. I just told you that, nigga!" Flip snapped.

"Aye, don't forget I'm still big cuz." J-Bo's voice was serious. He stepped closer to Flip.

"Okay, what the hell that supposed to mean?"

"It means I still deserve that respect, and I'll still whoop yo ass!"

Flip's seriousness was overpowered by a grin. "Got me fucked up!"

J-Bo laughed. "You know wassup wit me, lil nigga. You need anything?" J-Bo asked as he stretched out again. Flip shook his head. J-Bo programmed his number in Flip's phone, dapped him up, then he and Asia left.

"What was going on?" Asia asked, walking back to the truck.

"What you mean?" J-Bo was confused.

"When I walked back in the room, I felt some tension."

J-Bo got in the passenger seat and pulled the 9mm from under the seat, placing it on his lap.

"Aint shit, that's lil cuz. It's all love."

"I know it's all love," Asia said, getting in the car, starting the ignition. "But I know tension when I feel it." She looked at J-Bo's eyes. They were dark.

"Cuz just…" he stopped. "You know his girl, Daneisha?" His words were careful.

"Daneisha from Diamonds?" she asked, merging into traffic.

J-Bo shook his head. "Nah, you don't know her. I'm trippin'. They met online, while we was locked up."

"So what's the problem? She rode with him through a prison bid. She a real bitch."

J-Bo sighed. "I just want my lil cuz to have the best of everything, no cap."

"Where we going? And I still don't see the problem," Asia probed.

"Go back to the safe house. I'm finna see if Snag got any leads on where Tez nem might be. And I guess what I'm tryna say is, Daneisha cool and all, but she's…" he paused.

"What? What's wrong with her?"

"The bitch ugly as fuck. Big ass fucking horse teeth, ugly ass dreads, the bitch bout eight feet tall."

Looking at J-Bo, Asia could do nothing but bust out laughing. "You wrong, J-Bo."

Before he could reply, they heard a police siren. Then came the lights.

"They're behind me, J-Bo," Asia said.

"Don't panic," he said, pressing the button on the volume knob to make the hidden compartment under the seat open. He dropped the pistol in it, then pressed the button back to close it. Asia pulled over and the Atlanta PD squad car pulled up behind them. Putting the car in Park, they sat there in silence as the officer read their plates. They were on a main road, and cars were passing by going either way. Minutes later, the officer got out and approached them. Asia rolled her window down.

"License and registration," he said.

"Okay, that's cool. But why you pull us over?" J-Bo asked.

"I have my reasons," he said, staring at them suspiciously.

J-Bo grabbed the vehicle's registration from the glove compartment and handed it to Asia. She gave that, along with her driver's license, to the officer and he walked back to his car.

"Racist, Santa Claus lookin' mothafuckas," J-Bo mumbled.

The officer returned and gave the credentials back to Asia. He looked at J-Bo. "What about you?"

"What about me?"

"License?"

"I just got out yesterday. I'm on my way to the DMV, now."

"Step out the car."

"Fa fuckin what? I just got outta prison yesterday, nigga. I'm on my way to get a fuckin license now!"

"J-Bo, just step out, bra. These police been killin niggas and getting away with it," Asia whispered.

The officer placed his hand on his gun. "Step out the car!"

J-Bo stepped out and was handcuffed, frisked, and put in the back of the patrol car. Asia sat waiting for the officer to let J-Bo out, until she saw his car blend in with traffic.

Asia drove to Smoke's condo. Her key didn't work. She banged on the door.

"Who is it?"

"It's me! Open the door," she said. "Why the hell did you change the locks?" she asked when Smoke opened the door. Both of his eyes were still swollen, but they were opened.

"Why the fuck did you join Young Boss without asking me!" he snapped.

"Baby, I know you mad about that, but that has to wait."

"Wait? Nah, I packed all yo shit! Get it and get out!"

"J-Bo just got locked up!"

"What? For what?" he asked frantically.

"I don't know. We got pulled over and—"

"They find anythang in the car?" he cut her off.

"No."

Damn, Smoke thought. What the fuck goin' on?

***

"Sir, I'm not going to keep asking you for simple information. This is my last time. I need to know these things so we'll know where to place you. Now, are you straight, gay, bisexual, or transgender," the nice old lady asked J-Bo from the other side of the glass of the holding cell he was in.

"Bitch, fuck all dat! Why am I here?" J-Bo blared, spit flying from his mouth onto the glass.

She smiled. "For the disrespect and failure to cooperate, you'll be placed in protective custody." She walked away.

"Fuck you, bitch! Old, fat, nasty, stankin', bitch!"

"What's the problem, sir?" a younger, black officer asked J-Bo.

"Bra, these folks just locked me up and ain't tellin me shit. I don't know why the fuck I'm here. I just maxed out from ten years. No way in the fuck I'm in here!"

"Hold up." The officer walked to the desk, grabbed some papers, and returned.

"What's yo last name, man?" he asked, looking at his roster sheet.

"Dew," J-Bo answered.

"He got you for littering and failure to provide identification."

"He a mothafuckin lie! I ain't littered shit. I just left the hospital from seeing my lil cousin! Plus, refusing to identify yourself is not a crime in the state of Georgia," J-Bo informed.

"It's not a crime but it is a factor to be considered in a decision to arrest."

J-Bo shook his head. "So what I gotta do, man?"

"You'll see a first appearance judge in the morning. I'm sure they'll release you," the officer said and walked away.

Early the next morning the officer entered the dorm. "Y'all get ready for first appearance!" He called out to the men locked behind the door.

When J-Bo heard the officer's voice, he jumped up from his bed and started banging on the door. "I'm ready, man!"

"Who is that?" asked the officer.

"Jerome Dew!"

"What cell?"

J-Bo looked on the door for the cell number. "Sixteen!"

The officer came and opened J-Bo's door, searched him, cuffed him, and took him into the hallway.

"Why you so anxious?" the officer asked in the hallway.

"Because ain do shit. I just got out the otha day. Did ten fuckin years. Den y'all got me on fuckin PC, stuck in this fuckin room dat smell like shit," J-Bo spazzed.

The officer laughed. "Hopefully you'll be out of here soon." He looked at his clipboard. "Just waiting on one more."

"He need to hurry the fuck up," J-Bo mumbled.

There was knocking from the other side of the door. The officer unlocked the door and entered the dorm. He came back a few seconds later.

"Where da nigga at?" J-Bo asked in frustration.

"Obviously, y'all got some sorta beef, so y'all can't be out here together. I don't got time for a damn fight. C'mon."

He grabbed J-Bo by the arm and took him outside and placed him on one side of the police van.

"Ain't this some bullshit. We got beef," J-Bo laughed. "Prolly one of them bitch ass niggas I stabbed in prison seen me and got spooked," he thought aloud before laughing hard. *Can't wait to tell Flip bout this shit*, he thought.

They uncuffed J-Bo and placed him in a cell alone. The hallway held twelve rooms and each room held one inmate. He paced back and forth as the guard called names.

"Michael Willis!" an officer called out. Another officer went and got Mr. Willis out the cell and took him in the room before the judge. This process repeated itself with different names. J-Bo laid down on the single bench. The room was so small his head was right next to the toilet when he laid down. He got up and did some push-ups. He looked at all the gang tagging on the wall. He smiled when he seen GD and Young Boss had been tagged. He did another set of push-ups.

"Martez Challey!" the officer called.

Martez Challey, Martez Challey. *What the fuck*, J-Bo thought, jumping up from the bench, running to the door. *I know gotdamn well that ain't…*

His thoughts were interrupted when he looked out the small window and seen the officer escorting Tez into the courtroom.

"What the fuck!" J-Bo yelled.

Tez looked back then whispered something to the officer. After Tez was inside the room the officer came to J-Bo's door and put an all black flap over the window so he couldn't see out of it. J-Bo laughed. His hands started to fidget. His palms begin to sweat. His energy level was so high, he started swinging at the air as if he was fighting.

"Pussy, nigga!" He swung a punch. "Bitch!" He threw a jab. "Fuck, nigga!" He swung a right hook. He was preparing to drop and do some push-ups when the door opened.

"Dew, cuff up," the officer said.

J-Bo put his hands behind his back. He was looking in each cell as the officer escorted him to the end room.

"Keep your eyes straight," the officer said, jerking J-Bo's arm.

Inside the room, the judge's face was on a flat screen. He addressed J-Bo and read the officer's statement. J-Bo was being charged for allegedly throwing trash out of the car window on a main street, and refusing to provide identification. Ignoring the part about the trash, J-Bo told the judge he was never read his Miranda rights. Looking through the officer's statement, the judge saw that the officer didn't include reading J-Bo his Miranda rights. Not wanting to continue such a petty case, he granted J-Bo a signature bond.

Back at the jail, J-Bo was in the same intake room he started out in. They asked him if he had any personal items in his cell he needed to go get. He said no.

"I need to use the phone while I wait to sign my bond," J-Bo anxiously told the guard.

"Go right ahead," the officer said.

J-Bo dialed for Ken. "Hello," Ken answered.

You have a free prepaid call from... "J-Bo." J-Bo said his name. Press five to accept or eight to decline. Ken pressed five.

"J-Bo, what happened, bro? You aiight?" Ken asked.

"Ken, listen, big bra—"

"What you charged with?" Ken cut him off.

"Man, fuck dat, listen bra—"

Ken cut him off again. "What are you charged with?"

"Fuck da charge. Tez is here!" J-Bo barked into the phone. "I just seen his bitch ass at court! Hello? Ken?" The line was silent.

"Emergency lockdown! Everybody lock it down!" all the officer's yelled, rushing the inmates back into their cells.

"Hold up, man I'm finna bond out," J-Bo yelled to the officer.

"You'll have to wait until we come off of emergency lockdown," the officer yelled, before two of them wrestled to handcuff him and take him back into his cell.

CHAPTER 4

"Baby, get up," Smoke said, stretching out. He leaned up against the wooden headboard and stared at Asia peacefully sleeping on her stomach. "Get up," He said, smacking her on her juicy booty. He smiled when it jiggled. "Get cha light skinned ass up."

She jumped up. "What time is it?" She asked quickly.

Smoke looked at his phone. "Six."

She ran to the spacious bathroom to get herself together. Smoke started making the California king sized bed. After he finished, he walked in the closet and found her a simple outfit; blue jeans, a white long sleeve shirt, and some white air Force ones. He laid it on the bed and walked in the bathroom. Asia was brushing her teeth.

"Tell Ken what happened yesterday, and he'll tell you what to do," he stated.

"You not coming with me?" she asked after rinsing her mouth out.

"Nah, my face all beat up. I can't come out the house like this."

She rushed into the closet.

"Yo clothes on the bed, shawty," he said, stopping her.

She smiled. "Thanks baby," she said before quickly changing.

"Hurry up and handle that, cuz I can't get enough," he said looking at her butt.

"Nasty," she flirted.

"Fuck! I do gotta go," he said slipping on a simple outfit.

"Why?" she asked, sliding her feet into her shoes.

"At no point are you pose to be without a security escort."

When they pulled up to his house, Ken was in the driveway packing some bags into the trunk of his Ferrari. He stared at the SUV as it approached. Asia got out.

"Good morning," she greeted.

Ken looked at his watch. "What happened?"

"We were leaving the hospital from seeing Flip. We got pulled over. J-Bo got a lil smart with the police and they locked him up. I don't know what charge they tried to put on him."

"Have you checked the system for his name or called a bail bondsman?" he asked, agitated.

Asia shook her head.

"Ok, listen. You slippin'. That's the first thing you should've done. But, don't worry. Tez is in that jail with J-Bo. I want that jail surrounded twenty-four-seven. Do not let Tez get away. I want him dead." He closed the trunk and walked around to the driver's side. "Get J-Bo bonded out. You can pick up the money from anyone of the spots. I have to get to Texas right now. I have to sign some papers for my artist to continue working." He boarded the sports car and pulled off.

Back in the car, she gave Smoke the rundown on what Ken wanted to be done. They drove to the safe house. On the way there, Smoke made a call.

"Free at Last Bail Bonds on Peachtree, how may I help you?" a woman answered.

"Hey, um, I'm tryna see if somebody gotta bond," Smoke asked.

"This person was arrested in Atlanta, correct?" she clarified.

Smoke looked at Asia. She nodded, keeping her eyes on the road. "Yes," Smoke said.

"Name please?"

"Uhhhhh, Jermia- nah, Jerome Dew." He had to remember.

"Jerome Dew?"

"Yea."

"One second please." She put the phone down and started typing. "Okay, I see he was granted a signature bond. So, he won't have to physically come here. He can just sign from the jail, and he'll be released," she informed.

"How long ago was this?" Smoke asked.

"About two hours ago."

Smoke hung up. "If he got a signature bond two hours ago, why the fuck he ain't out?"

"He might be, baby. He left his phone here." She pointed to the glove compartment. They drove to the safe house and had Snag drive one of the few Young Boss whips to follow them.

"Call Snag and ask him where's Ty-Ty," Smoke commanded.

"I don't have the number," she said.

Smoke dialed the number on his phone and gave it to her.

"I'm right behind you, bra," Snag answered.

"This Asia, where's Ty-Ty?"

"Oh my bad, sis. I think he in Pittsburgh."

"Go get him." She looked at Smoke. He shot her a thumbs up. "Go get him and meet us by the jail." She looked at Smoke again. He quietly told her to hang up. She did.

"That's how you get niggas to respect yo position," he said.

"How? By being rude as hell?" she asked.

"Nah. By statin' the business and hangin' up. Leave a nigga no room to negotiate or nun."

Asia smiled and occasionally looked at Smoke as she drove. She took her right hand off the wheel and grabbed his left palm, and they squeezed hands. She continued steering with her left. "You still mad at me for joining without talking to you first?" she asked.

"Nah, it's cool. Ain stuttin nat shit," he said before gently kissing her hand with his swollen lips. "Stop at a beauty supply," he said.

Without any questions, she stopped. "What we need out of here, bae?" she asked.

"Grab four black ski masks. The long kind that can roll up and look like a skully," he stated.

She got out of the car and went into the salon.

Thirty minutes later they all met up at a burned down abandoned house on Warfield Street, in Southwest Atlanta. Snag and Ty-Ty parked behind Asia and Smoke. Smoke called Snag and told them to come to the truck he and Asia were in.

"You remember what I told you?" Smoke asked, as the two approached their truck.

"Yea, I remember. I got it, bae," Asia said, rolling down her window. She handed two of the ski masks to Snag. Snag gave Ty-Ty one. Already knowing the drill, they rolled it up and put it on as a skull cap. "Snag, I want you to walk back and forth down Tilden Street. Me and Smoke going to ride back and forth up Rice. And Ty-Ty, I need you riding back and forth down Jefferson. Tez is a skinny black ass nigga. Our goal is to snatch him up. If he make shit too hot with trying to run or wateva," she hesitated. Smoke discreetly poked her back. "Then kill him," she finally said.

"You want a nigga to pop him right out here? On these hot ass streets next to the jail?" Ty-Ty asked aggressively.

"Yea, that's what she said, nigga. She a grown boss! You betta respect rank, or yo ass will get dealt with right out here on these hot ass streets next to the jail," Smoke said, leaning up from the passenger seat. Smoke gave Ty-Ty a solid stare so mean it would scare a tiger off.

"Tez is in this jail. I'm about to find out for what, so we'll know how long to be out here," Asia said, pulling out her phone.

"You don't even know what he in for? This shit could be a blank mission," Snag said.

Smoke hit the glove compartment button and grabbed the pistol from under the seat. "Y'all niggas tryin' her because she a female! But disrespect rank one more mothafuckin time, and I'm a start shootin," Smoke snapped.

"Baby, chill…" Asia started.

"Nah, don't tell me to fuckin chill," he said, staring at the two men.

They all dropped their heads when an ambulance followed by a police cruiser came flying past them from the jail.

Snag smiled, exposing his two missing front teeth. "Make sure you respect rank, Smoke," Snag said as he and Ty-Ty walked off.

"Fuck niggas be tryin' shit to see who gone go for it," Smoke said aggressively, as they began to blend onto Rice Street.

"I need you to heal up, Smoke. Can you get in more trouble for threatening them?" she asked. Her eyes grew big as she silently worried about Smoke getting another beating.

"Naw, respecting rank is mandatory. I coulda shot both of them niggas on the spot and would'na been in no trouble. One thang I can say bout that big swole mothafucka, Ken. He don't tolerate no form of disrespect."

"What's his name again?" she asked, pressing the dial button.

"Just drive. I got this," he said, taking the phone from her.

"Fulton County Jail, deputy Ward speaking."

"I'm tryna see what's my brother's charge and if he got a bond," Smoke said.

"Name please?"

"Martez Challey."

"Yes sir. He's in for failure to appear in court. He received a signature bond today."

"Has he left yet?" Smoke asked.

"Uhhh, sir, I can't provide you with those details," said the deputy.

Smoke ended the line. "His bitch ass still there," he mumbled.

***

"Dew!" The same officer called J-Bo, as he approached his cell.

"Man, get me tha fuck outta here!" J-Bo's voice shook the walls.

"Ahh, shut up, crybaby. We had a code!" The officer unlocked his cell and escorted him down to booking. "Full house, huh?" the officer said as they entered the booking area, and all seventy-five chairs were full of new intakes.

"Let me use the phone real quick," J-Bo asked.

"Either the phone or yo release papers, which one?" the officer asked.

"Man, it ain't even nobody at the desk right now. Damn, just give a nigga like two minutes," he complained.

The officer waved him off and went looking for the clerk to process J-Bo's paperwork.

J-Bo shot to the wall phone, and quickly dialed Ken's number

"Pick up, Ken... c'mon, man, fuck!" He slammed the phone on the wall receiver when Ken didn't answer. He tried again to no avail. "Fuck!" He slammed the phone again.

"Hey you! Slam that fuckin phone one more time and I'll charge your ass with destruction of government property," the officer yelled, coming from behind the counter with the clerk.

"My bad, man, just let me make one more call."

"If you dial one more number, I promise, I'm going to process all these people first," the officer said, pointing to all the new intakes.

J-Bo hung up the phone and approached the counter. His papers were laid out in front of him.

"Sign here, here, and there," the officer said. After signing, he made a copy for J-Bo, filed the original one, and walked J-Bo to the door.

"Aye, what da hell was the emergency?" asked J-Bo.

"You want to go home, don't you?" the officer asked sternly.

"I'm talkin' bout lockdown. Them dum-ass niggas in the dorm talkin' bout somebody kilt theyself. That shit true?"

The officer used his key card to unlock the exit door. "That mothafucka wasn't trying to kill himself," he laughed. "Acting like he was hanging from that weak ass sheet. If it was up to me, I'da let his ass hang. He wanted some attention or he wanted a free ride to the damn hospital," the officer explained.

"Who was it?" J-Bo was curious.

***

Smoke's phone rung. "Yo?" he answered. He hung up. "Warfield Street!" he barked. Asia hit a U-turn as quick as she could and stepped on the pedal.

"They got him?" Asia asked frantically, halfway smiling.

"Snag say somebody with a hoodie and a facemask on coming his way from the jail." Smoke elaborated the message while cocking the head of the gun back.

This million gone do me and bae real good right about now, Smoke thought.

***

After getting the call, Ty-Ty added acceleration to the truck. He made a sharp right turn off Jefferson, turning onto Marietta Boulevard, mashing the gas far as it would go as the street converted into Rice.

About fifty feet away, Snag snatched his hat down, turning it into a ski mask. He stuck his hand into his pocket, pulling at the butt of his 9mm. The man with the hoodie on saw Snag clutching and took off running.

Asia turned hard on Warfield, flooring it. Snag was running towards the truck. She made a quick hard stop that would have sent them both through the windshield if not for the seatbelts. Smoke handed her the pistol.

"Go! Be careful! Go!" Smoke yelled. Asia quickly exited the truck and begin running towards Snag. Snag was pointing towards the houses on the side street.

"Foster!" Snag yelled, not slowing down. Asia ran with him through some raggedy houses towards Foster Place Street.

Smoke threw the truck in reverse. He drove like that to the end of the street, then made a quick left drift onto Rice Street, still driving backwards until he blocked the only way off Foster Place.

Yea, mothafucka, come on, he thought seeing a hooded man running towards him. He hit the button on the volume knob to open the compartment under his seat. He pulled the gun, rolled the passenger window down with a switch on the driver's door, and took aim at the running man.

***

Soon as Ty-Ty was going good and fast on Rice Street, the SUV Asia was driving came turning fast, driving backwards. Ty-Ty hurriedly stepped on the brakes, sending his head hitting the wheel. He hopped out the vehicle with his weapon loaded and sprinted towards the running man. The hooded man slowed up when he saw he had nowhere to go.

Getting closer to the end of the street, he noticed the trucks. He came to a complete stop, breathing hard.

"Get dat ass in this truck, Tez!" Smoke called out as the rest of the crew closed in on him.

He pulled the hoodie back. "Nigga, it's me!" J-Bo barked before jumping in the passenger seat of the truck with Smoke. Asia and Snag jumped in the backseat. Ty-Ty ran back to the abandoned truck.

"Where Tez?" Smoke asked, looking around.

"That mothafucka!" J-Bo paused for a deep breath. "Pulled a mental health stunt, actin like he tryna hang his self," he said, with another pause to catch his breath.

"Why would he do that?" Asia asked from the back. Snag was also out of breath. Asia seemed fine.

"So, they'll have to send him out to the hospital to see a mental health doctor. Niggas in jail do shit like dat all the time. He. . . seen me at court today. He knew he had to get the fuck outta here," J-Bo said.

"Damn, he smart. But why you was running bra? I just knew you was Tez," said Snag.

"I was runnin because I seen a nigga with a mask on, clutching a burner walkin' towards me....Smoke, get us the fuck outta here!"

CHAPTER 5

"Can I speak to nurse Lisa?" J-Bo asked over the phone.

"Sure, who's calling?" asked the receptionist.

"Malcolm," he answered.

"One second, please." She put the phone down. Moments passed, leaving nothing but the sounds of hospital activity to be heard in the background until the phone could be heard moving as it was picked up.

"Nurse Lisa," she answered.

"Wassup, my baby," J-Bo smiled.

"Umm, who is this?" She sounded confounded.

"J-Bo," he said smoothly.

"Oh, shit, J-Bo!" She was quietly excited. "I haven't heard from you in like a month. It's almost time to come home, right? I want to pick you up from the airport."

"I'm already home—"

She cut him off. "Oh my God, I want to see you... like today. I get off at eight."

Lisa was a random chick J-Bo had met on a dating app called Plenty of Fish while he was locked up. Just a late night bored phone sex type of thing. Nothing major, and he'd never led her to believe otherwise, either. It wasn't like she had held him down, or they had got some money together. Would he fuck? Yea, but he had just done a decade behind the wall. His mind was on a bag.

"Alright, cool. But I need yo help real quick, shawty."

"What you need?" she quickly answered.

"Martez Challey, look 'em up. Let me know if he there."

"I think that's the boy that just came in from the county jail..."

"Yea, that's him. I just need to know when he's gettin' ready to be discharged."

"Okay, I'll let you know. I have to get back to work, baby. Give me your number."

"What now?" Smoke asked, parking in front of the safe house. Ty-Ty parked behind him. J-Bo got out the truck and stretched out. He stood in the open doorway.

"You go home and rest. Put some ice or sum on yo face. Shit look bad," J-Bo told Smoke. "I'm finna slide off with Ty-Ty for a minute. Asia and Snag, just keep y'all eyes open for anything dat can get us closer to Tez and Nae. I want that fuckin' money. Don't go too far from the hospital just in case I need one of y'all to slide," he said before walking away.

"J-Bo!" Asia called behind him. He turned around. "I just remembered. Nae owns a salon not too far from here. Want me to go look around?" she asked.

"Yea, if you don't find nun, burn dat bitch down," he said before walking off.

"Headed to that shop Nae work at?" Smoke asked, when Asia got in the passenger.

"J-Bo said you need to go home and rest, bro," Snag said from the back seat.

Asia and Smoke locked eyes for a few seconds before Smoke drifted into traffic.

***

Snag took the wheel after dropping Smoke off. Asia gave him directions on where the salon was on Austell Road. They turned into the strip plaza. There was a Big Lots, a Dollar General, Nae's Beauty Salon, and a store on the end that appeared abandoned.

"What tha fuck?" said Snag, parking in front of the Dollar General.

"What?" Asia asked, looking around the plaza, thinking she's missing something.

"You said she owns this place," Snag asked, pointing to the salon.

"Yea, why?"

Snag turned the engine off. "This shit might be easier than we thought."

"What you mean?" She stared at the salon.

"This shit still runnin'," he said, watching a girl entering the salon. "That means somebody is in touch with the owner still." He made sense of it all.

"Ohhhhhh!" Asia threw her head against the seat. "I get it."

"I say we just run in that bitch and lay mothafuckas down!"

"No, Snag, are you crazy?" Asia retorted quickly. "We'll run in there. Just give me a lil time to put it together. This ain't Atlanta. Yo ass will go to jail fucking around in Cobb."

"Yea," Snag said, looking in her eyes. The moment almost felt awkward, at least to her.

"Um, let's get outta here. Let's go linger around by the hospital just in case Tez show his face," Asia said.

***

A few hours later, J-Bo called the hospital back and got Nurse Lisa on the phone. He felt as if she was acting very weird. She wasn't answering questions straight up as usual and she was stuttering. She finally told him her shift ended in about twenty minutes and she'd give him a call the minute she clocks out.

***

"How long you and Smoke been together?" Snag asked, as he drove.

"A couple years," Asia answered. *Why the fuck does that matter?* She wondered.

"You used to dance, right?" Snag continued, looking at her like she was a snack.

She simply nodded her head and started texting Smoke.

"You know, since you a grown boss, we can pull up on any of the spots and have some of the young niggas do this shit. And we just take the credit for it later," he smiled, showing the open area.

"No, it's alright. I like to be out here doing this. It's the best way to learn."

And what the fuck kind of nigga want other people to put in yo fucking work and you take credit for it? That seem like some crab ass slimy shit, Asia thought.

"How come you haven't went and got your teeth fixed... or your skin?" she asked. Snag had small boils and acne of some sort covering his face. "I'm not trying to be rude or funny," she said, hoping she didn't offend him.

"Nah, it's cool. I'm..." he said, before swallowing hard. "You know what happened to my teeth? And my skin?" he asked, staying focused on the road.

"No, what?"

"I was doing security for one of the brother's a few years ago. While we were driving, somebody started shooting through the car. I jumped on the brother, protecting him from the bullets. I lost two teeth, and the heat from the bullets burned my face up. I never got it fixed as a reminder of how much love I really have for Young Boss," he explained.

Damn! I feel bad, Asia thought.

***

"Yo?" J-Bo answered.

"Hey, baby. Uh, it's Lisa, can you come by my place? I don't stay too far from the hospital."

J-Bo frowned. *This bitch sound funny*, J-Bo thought. "Yea, text me the address."

"You good?" Ty-Ty asked, pulling his gun from under the seat.

"Yea, dis my lil bitch house. I met her on POF when I was locked up. She sounded a lil weird just then. Ion know what she on," J-Bo responded, shrugging his shoulders.

The address came through, and J-Bo put it in the GPS app on his phone and gave Ty-Ty directions to Lisa's spot. Before long, they were pulling up.

"You want me to come in?" Ty-Ty asked.

"Nah, but get out the car," J-Bo said before getting out himself and going to the door.

He knocked, and Lisa opened the door, wearing a nightgown. She was an amazon thick woman. Her skin was like milk. Her hair stopped at her ass. She was about an inch taller than J-Bo. She hugged him quickly, looked around outside, pulled him in and closed the door.

"Okay, what the hell is going on?" Lisa asked, her voice innocent. Her house was simply lit by a few vanilla smelling candles. R. Kelly played in the speakers. *I'm finna fuck this bitch good*, J-Bo thought, looking at her ass poke.

"Who is that man standing outside?" she asked, looking out the window beside the door.

"He good. He my security," J-Bo said, reaching for her gown.

She swatted his hand away. "You told me when you get out, that life is behind you. Said you not with none of that crazy shit, right?" she frowned.

"I'm chillin. I'm not doin' nun crazy!" He exclaimed.

"Jerome, don't fucking insult my intelligence. Why did you need to know when that man was discharged today, huh? Why?" she questioned, placing a hand in her hip.

J-Bo leaned against the door. "That's my people. I wanted to have him a ride ready." He dropped his head, looking to the pretty tan carpet.

"Oh, your people, huh? But twenty minutes after you called and asked me that, a fucking attorney called asking for me." She emphasized the word 'me'. "I get on the fucking phone, and she goes to telling me that she is the mother fucker from the county jail lawyer, and she's been tipped that I might be releasing information about her client to people and asked me not to do it because his life is in danger and I could be charged with this and that," She paused for a deep breath. "So how the fuck would a damn lawyer know to call and tell me that?"

J-Bo rubbed his beard. How the fuck could dat even be possible? Who the fuck heard me talkin' to da bitch? Smoke? Nah, I know Smoke ain't said shit. Asia? Uh, shit Ion know. Snag? Snag ass is a lil weird but Ion think he would say nun. Ty-Ty? He wasn't in the truck with us, so he don't know shit about me talkin' to the bitch, J-Bo thought.

"Hello?" Lisa called, stepping closer to J-Bo.

"Ion know, baby." His vision was still drifted off. "I called you in front of the bro's, but ain think it was somethin' I had to hide and do," J-Bo explained, not wanting her to ever think he was trying to set her up in any kind of way.

"Well, looks like one of your bro's are some fucking snitches that could've costed me my job, probably my freedom," she stepped closer.

"What the fuck?" J-Bo whispered. *This shit just ain't making sense*, he thought. "Martez still there?" he asked.

"No," she answered, leaning towards J-Bo's face.

"He went back to the jail?"

"No, he had a bond already, so they released him from the hospital," she said and slightly kissed J-Bo lips. She tried to get a more firm grip of his lips but he turned and walked to the door."Wait. Where are you going?" Lisa watched him open the door. "J-Bo?"

He walked out and slammed the door behind him.

"J-Bo!"

***

"That was J-Bo. He said we're good for the night. Said we can call it a night and be ready to start looking tomorrow," Asia told Snag, as he drove aimlessly around the hospital area. They'd passed the hospital at least six times.

"Okay, cool, you hungry?" Snag asked, looking at her.

"Umm, yea, I am kinda hungry," she answered.

"J-Bo didn't say nothing specific?" he asked.

"Nope, just said we done for the night."

Snag's phone rung. "Wasup baby," he answered. "Oh naw, you good. Nothing to worry about. Haha, Okay. I'll see you tomorrow. Love you," he said and hung up.

"You got a girlfriend?" Asia asked, smiling hard.

Snag giggled. "Lil sum sum," he answered.

***

"Ty-Ty, when I jumped in the truck with Smoke and them over by the jail, I called dis nurse I know and told her to let me know when Tez gettin' discharged," J-Bo said, staring out the window as Ty-Ty drove. His fingers were still dancing through his beard. "Bitch, just told me the reason she ain't let me know is because a lawyer called her at work and told her not to release any of her client info or she'll be charged."

"But how the hell could a lawyer know that you asked her to let you know when he's being discharged?" Ty-Ty retorted.

"My fuckin point!" J-Bo slapped the armrest.

CHAPTER 6

After a serious, realist type of discussion, the two men started addressing realities, no corners to be cut at no point. Then they discovered something.

"That shit sound flakey as fuck," Ty-Ty said, as he rolled out of the driveway, cruising onto the dark street.

J-Bo nodded. "Exactly, bra. Ion get how something I said in front of our people could be repeated by anyone." J-Bo racked his brain as he gently tapped on the window.

"Yea, that shit strange. But maybe, the nigga had already put his lawyer on point. So that's why they called," said Ty-Ty.

"Even if that was true, how da fuck the lawyer know who to ask for, shawty?"

"You said shawty name in front of the guys?" asked Ty-Ty.

"Yea, shid, ain see no reason not too," J-Bo answered.

"Somebody talkin', fam," Ty-Ty said.

"But talkin' to who?" J-Bo wondered. "Who tryna protect Tez except Nae?"

Ty-Ty stopped at the red light. He looked over to J-Bo.

"I see what you saying, my nigga. But do you see what I'm sayin'?" Ty-Ty didn't break eye contact.

"So, who you thank talkin'?" J-Bo asked reluctantly.

"It could only be one of three people, fam." Ty-Ty turned his attention back to the road when the light turned green.

"But who you thank whoeva is talkin', is talkin' to?" J-Bo asked, overthinking.

Ty-Ty shrugged his shoulders and drove in silence.

***

"Soooo," Asia said. "Let's just say we were to run across Nae and Tez, right now—"

"I'ma kill 'em," Snag cut her off. He chuckled at the thought of running across the two while he was a few minutes away from Smoke's condo. He drifted off in his thoughts for a while, thinking how he would kill them.

Asia laughed. "I'm saying, what would you do with your million?" she asked.

"My million?" Snag raised an eyebrow. "If I kill them right now, I'll have two million."

"But, we've been looking for them together. So I'll get one million, right?"

Snag laughed. "Yea, if you shoot one of they ass. But I wouldn't leave you hangin' like that. I'd fuck with you on like ten dollars or so," he laughed. Asia didn't find that funny. Snag's phone rang. He looked at it then put it back down and let it continue to ring.

***

Smoke was already in bed by the time Asia entered the condo. It was dark. She maneuvered around the plush sectional that wrapped around the living room, and almost tripped over one of Smoke's Timberland's. She laughed, thinking how he just kicks his shoes off anywhere. She hit the shower then climbed in bed beside him.

"You up?" She gently rubbed a finger against his face.

"Yea, you know ain goin' to sleep without you coming home," he whispered.

"You been using ice?" She noticed the swollen area was going down.

"Yea."

"Want me to start squeezing some of this pus out?"

"Nah, just leave it. Let it heal on its own." He turned his face away from her fingers.

She gently kissed his face. "I find Snag to be a lil strange, bae," she said, laying her head on Smoke's chest.

Her hair pulled into a bun, was right in his face. He turned his head the other way.

"Yea, he's definitely off a lil bit," Smoke said, rubbing her shoulder. "He said something outta line?"

Should I tell him this nigga asked do I dance and how long me and him been together? she thought. "No, he didn't say nothing out of line, baby. He just seems a lil weird. And his phone rung a couple times. He ignored it. It's probably nothing."

"Yea, he been doing lil weird shit. He done been under investigation bout five times, but they never found nothing on him. And he's a big, big trick," Smoke smiled.

"Wait a minute, what? What you mean a big trick?" she laughed.

"He don't mind payin' for it." Smoke shook his head. "His ass ain't learned his lesson from fuckin' with Nae." He shook his head.

Asia frowned. "What you mean, baby?" She was confused.

"That's how dat nigga lost them teeth. He didn't know Nae was Ken's bitch, and tried to fuck her. Offered her a couple hundred dollars. She told him to just leave her alone but he kept trying until she told Ken. And shiiid, Ken ordered one of them twelve minute ass whoopins that I got," he chuckled. "And he lost two teeth."

"What about his skin?" she asked.

"Ion know. I think bra was in a fire when he was a kid or something."

Wow! This bitch ass nigga really lied, talking about he was protecting somebody from a bullet, Asia thought.

The next morning, Asia awakened, still lying in bed, tangled up in her thoughts. Why the fuck would Snag lie about how he lost his teeth? I mean, I'm sure nobody wants to admit being a trick. But why go in depth into that deep ass story of telling me what happened and come to find out, it's all a damn lie? Asia thought. She rolled over and Smoke's body wasn't there. In the air was some sort of blueberry aroma, so she assumed he was cooking. She rolled back over on the big soft Gucci pillows.

Smoke entered the room with two plates; two blueberry pancakes on each, a few bacon strips, scrambled eggs, and two glasses of orange juice.

"Wake dat ass up," Smoke said, entering the room. He laid the breakfast tray down in the center of the queen size bed and sat across from Asia. She stretched and yawned.

"Thank you, daddy," she murmured.

He nodded, cutting into the pancakes. "J-Bo gave y'all an agenda today?"

She took a baby sip of orange juice. "Nope, but we're planning on following one of them girls that work in that shop today," she said, before nibbling on a bacon strip.

Smoke looked at her. "Follow a girl and then do what?" He squinted his eyes.

Asia cut into her pancakes. "Just see where she goes. See if she'll lead us to Nae or Tez."

Smoke took a deep breath.

"What baby?" she asked.

"I love Young Boss to death. But I swear I hate that you joined this shit. It's dangerous as fuck, shawty!" He shook his head, and sipped his juice.

"This part isn't dangerous, Smoke. All we're doing is seeing where she goes then we're out of there. I promise," she explained.

"It don't always work like that." His facial expression was firm.

She sucked her teeth. "Gotdamn, Smoke!" She dropped her silver spoon in the eggs on the glass plate. "How could just following a bitch to see where she takes us go wrong? Huh? How?"

"How could it go wrong? Are you fuckin serious?" he barked.

"Yes, I'm serious! How?" she yelled, frustrated with Smoke.

"Okay, smart ass! What if you go following a bitch. She knows she's being followed but called Tez and let him know she being followed. Then he tells her to keep coming. So now you give him the advantage to lay on y'all and hop out the fuckin bushes somewhere shootin'!"

"Not gonna fucking happen," Asia said, going into the bathroom and slamming the door.

***

"Slide over," Asia said, as she approached the SUV waiting for her in the parking lot. Snag slid over to the passenger and let her take the wheel.

"Oh, you wanna drive today, huh?" asked Snag.

"Yea, I'm anxious right now, man. I need a fucking black or something." She turned into the first gas station she saw and purchased a box of wine Black & Mild's. Snag took the pack, freaked the black, lit it, hit it once, and then gave it to her.

"Thank you, bra." She smiled, happy he knew to do what she couldn't do, and drive at the same time. Snag fired him one of the black's up also and put on Psycho's new song.

Pulling into the partially filled parking lot, Asia, slowed up, perfectly turning into an open space directly in front of the Dollar store. She was close enough to Nae's salon where she could see through the glass. Asia used the automatic button to make the small sunroof in the ceiling slide back and she looked up.

"What you lookin' at?" Snag asked, trying to follow her eyes.

"The clouds," she said, not breaking her focus.

"You like the clouds?" he asked, almost wanting to laugh.

"Yea, me and my cousin, Tiffany," she paused at the mention of Tiffany's name. "Me and her both love nature. Our foster mom used to have us around all kinds of nature."

"Ain know you and Tiffany was cousins. I just thought that was a scene for the stage." Snag was surprised.

Asia slightly chuckled. "Nah, her black ass is my cousin. I don't know how that girl got that black, but she's sexy." Asia laughed.

"Hell yea, both of y'all is." Snag slid it in there.

Asia looked at him and rolled her eyes.

"Oh shit, we got somebody leavin', What time you got?" Snag said, zooming his vision closer on the girl coming out the store.

"It's six. We got thirty more minutes before they close," Asia answered, locking in.

"What dat pose to mean? Let's follow her ass now." He watched her like a hungry lion watches its prey.

"No! If she's not the last one to leave, she could just be some peon help that doesn't know shit. Now, we get the bitch that's locking the place up, we know she'll know something," she elaborated.

"Okay, here we go," Snag said, watching another girl come out and lock the door. She was a heavy-set black girl; kind of favored a sumo wrestler. She wobbled to her car, a small burgundy Toyota, and climbed in. The driver side seemed to drop when she sat down. Closing the door, she crunk up the car, backed out, pulled off to the plaza exit, and turned right mixing into traffic.

They followed her around for about an hour. Then finally, she turned into a residential area in North Atlanta. There was a house for rent a few houses over, and across the street. Snag got out and took the sign down and Asia parked there.

"Wanna run in dat mothafucka?" Snag asked, after waiting for an hour.

"No, just chill out," Asia said, looking around as the sun dropped more and more. She couldn't stop thinking about Smoke's logic. *What if this is a set-up? What if we're exactly where Tez wants us?* Asia hit the button on the volume knob to open the spots under the seats. She pulled the regulation 9mm that was always there and laid it on her lap.

"What's up? What's going on?" Snag snatched the 9 from under his seat and watched the windows like a hawk.

"Nothing, I just. . . Nothing, just forget it." She looked in her rearview.

"How bout you call Smoke to come get you, and I sit here and plot all night. Ion want you out here stressin' and worryin' and shit," he suggested. She refused at first, but she knew it made more sense that way.

She pulled out her phone and called Smoke.

***

After being home with Smoke for a few hours and a few hot sessions of nasty, unprotected sex, Asia still had energy. "I can't sleep," she thought aloud. She had to shower because Smoke had came in her mouth a few times and some of his nut got in her hair. Smoke was knocked out. She called Snag after her shower and got no answer. *I hope he's alright,* she thought. So, she decided to go check on him. She moved swiftly through the condo, being sure not to awaken Smoke. She knew he would probably have an attitude about her wanting to go check in on Snag in the middle of the night.

Moving quickly, she put her hair in a ponytail, threw on some leggins, an oversized graphic tee, and a pair of Tasman Uggz. She grabbed Smoke's keys off the kitchen counter, and making her way to the door, one of his black hoodies caught her attention laying on the back of one of the living room couches.

This might come in handy, she thought, grabbing it and walking out the front door.

Fifteen minutes later, she parked in the front of the subdivision, and took the 9mm Smoke kept in his car and tucked it in the hoodie pocket. She went walking up the street towards the house. *There he go*, she thought, seeing the truck in the same spot she parked it in just hours ago. She crept on the side of the bushes, avoiding the street lights coming off the buildings. Once on the other side of the truck, she used both hands on the window to see inside. No one. She checked the back windows. No one. *Where the fuck is Snag*, she thought.

Asia stood still beside the truck for a few minutes. Slowly, she scanned the area, hoping Snag would be taking a leak in a bush somewhere. But he wasn't. The air was cool. Cool to the point you're not cold, but if you stand outside long enough, you'll get cold. She stretched the drawstrings hanging from Smoke's black hoodie she had on. It's was unisex so you couldn't tell it belonged to Smoke. It fit her slightly larger, but not noticeably. She approached the house in which they saw the girl enter. It was a pink, two story home, with a three-car garage. The lawn was about a week overdue for mowing. She pulled the gun out, holding it upwards as she made her way around the front of the house. She slowly peaked around the corner with the tip of the gun, looking first like they do in the movies.

She was about to try the backyard, even with the wooden fencing, but the *BEWARE OF DOG* sign gave her a change of mind. She peeped through the small garage windows. The Toyota was there. *What if Tez them got Snag inside tied up or some shit?* Asia's anxiety made her wonder all kinds of shit. She got to the front door and put her hand on the knob. The instant she touched it, her heart skipped a beat. Sweat beads formed on her forehead and under her armpits. Slowly, she turned the knob but the door was locked.

Shit, she thought.

She crept to the two windows in front of the house, but couldn't see anything but white blinds through one window. And the other, through just a tiny crack in a blind, she was able to see a quiet, dark house.

Where the fuck is this nigga, she thought.

Running back to the truck she tried calling him again. No answer. She tried to open the doors but they were all locked. *Fuck this shit*, she thought, running towards the front of the subdivision. She was parked in the driveway of a home that was for rent. Getting inside the car, she rubbed her hands together. She cranked the engine, turned the heat on low, and called Smoke.

"Where da fuck you at, shawty?" he answered, sleepily.

"Baby, I had a feeling something wasn't right with Snag. I came out here. Baby, this nigga is fucking missing!" She tried keeping her voice down.

"Missin'?" He rubbed his eyes, sounding more alive.

"Yes, the truck is still here, but he's not," she explained.

"Well, you da grown boss, so what next?" Smoke asked.

Asia sighed. "Get yo ass here and bring somebody with you."

"Bring somebody for?"

"I want this fucking door kicked," Asia stated.

Half hour later, Smoke and Ty-Ty were pulling in next to Asia. She got out Smoke's truck and got into the one Ty-Ty whipped up in. Soon as her door was closed Smoke turned around, lifted his ski mask and kissed her on the lips. Ty-Ty wore a ski mask also.

"You alright, sis?" asked Ty-Ty.

"Yea, I'm alright. I don't think Snag is, though."

"Tell us from beginning to end again," said Smoke. He used a bandana to wipe the 9mm off. After Asia finished telling her story they were ready to rock out.

"Baby, grab my otha gun out my truck," Smoke said.

"I already got it," she said, holding it up. "I'll drive," she said, getting out the back. Ty-Ty hopped in the back, and she hopped in, put the truck in Drive and pulled slowly down the street.

They passed a four-way in the neighborhood and the truck was filled with light from the high beams of a car that turned onto the street behind them just as they passed.

Smoke looked back. "The fuck?"

Red and blue lights bounced around the inside of the truck as they came to life on the top of the car behind them. It was the police.

"Fuck! It's 12!" Ty-Ty groaned.

"I got this." Calmly, Asia pulled curbside, and hit the button on the volume knob. The compartments opened and they all dropped their burners under the seats. Smoke and Ty-Ty removed their ski-masks and dropped them in the compartments, too. She hit the button again to close the spot.

The officer pulled to a stop behind them, got out and approached the driver side. Asia rolled the window down.

"Ma'am," the old, Steven Seagal look-alike officer shined his flashlight throughout the truck. He placed his hand on his gun. "What y'all doing out here so late?"

"We're thinking about buying a house in this neighborhood and wanted to see how it is during the wee hours," Asia lied.

The officer suspiciously eyed Smoke and Ty-Ty. "License and registration," he said. Asia slowly handed them to him, and he walked back to his squad car.

Ty-Ty watched him from the rearview mirror. "Aye, Smoke."

"Yea."

"We might need to get the fuck on."

"You can. I'm not leavin' Asia."

Ty-Ty was thinkin' she could just run with them, but thought better of it. "Damn, you dead ass right, bra. And I ain't leavin' if y'all aint. However this shit play out, it is what it is."

"Fasho."

Minutes passed that felt like hours, and before long, Steven Seagal was walking back. Stopping at Asia's window, he leaned down.

"Well, ma'am." He looked at Smoke and Ty-Ty, then back to Asia. "Everything checked out." He gave her the credentials back with a smile. "Yall drive safe, and try not to be out here too late. People 'round these parts ain't used to seeing cars cruising through late night. Might make 'em suspicious. Wouldn't want you getting stopped again."

Asia returned his smile. "Yea, sure thing."

He nodded towards Smoke and Ty-Ty. "Alright, fellas. Enjoy the rest of your night."

"Aiight, you do the same sir," Ty-Ty said.

Steven Seagal walked back to his squad car, got in and did a U-turn. Asia looked at Smoke, then at Ty-Ty. Both of the men's facial expression read *what the fuck!*

Asia pressed the button on the volume knob, and everybody grabbed their pieces when the spots in the floor slid open. Smoke and Ty-Ty grabbed their ski-masks and pulled them down over their heads.

"Kick the door. I'm sure Snag is in there," Asia said, slightly stepping on the pedal.

Smoke looked back at Ty-Ty. "You already know how we do. We shoot at all movement dat we can't identify."

Ty-Ty nodded.

Asia stopped the truck directly behind where Snag was supposed to be.

"Right there," Asia pointed. "You can't really see because it's dark, but the house is a light pink."

"The one wit dat brown fence?" Smoke asked, looking through the windshield.

She nodded. "Yea, baby. That's the one."

Stepping out the truck, Smoke and Ty-Ty jogged across the street to the house, running low, trying to dodge anyone that might just so happened to be peeping out their window. As they positioned themselves around the house Asia got out the truck. Stretching her legs, she approached the other truck and used two hands to look through the driver's side window, and there was Snag. His seat was leaned back, and he was sleeping.

Asia turned and ran towards the house. Ty-Ty's thick leg was off the ground and in motion, ready to kick. Smoke stood beside him with his weapon trained on the door.

"He's in the car," she said, in a loud whisper. Ty-Ty dropped his leg. Startled, Smoke swung around, weapon on her. He lowered it quickly when he saw who it was.

"I thought you said he wasn't in the car?" he loudly whispered back.

"He wasn't," she answered. The three of them crossed the street again. Ty-Ty snatched at the door handle, but it was locked. He knocked on the glass three times and Snag jumped. Realizing who it was, he opened his door.

"What the hell happened to you? I was worried," said Asia.

"Ain't nothin happen to me. What you mean?" He looked around.

"I came back to check on you." She scratched her ponytail. "Not too long ago and you wasn't here."

Snag frowned. "I've been right here da whole time, sis," he said matter-of-factly.

Asia slowly shook her head. "Snag, you were not in this truck about twenty or thirty minutes ago." Her soft voice had turned rough.

Snag grinned. "I promise on my dead brotha I was."

I can't believe this nigga is lying like this, Asia thought, staring at him.

CHAPTER 7

"Baby," Asia said from the back seat. "Ty-Ty."

"Yea?" Smoke answered.

"Wassup, sis?" Ty-Ty answered.

"On Young Boss, that nigga lying," she declared.

Silence.

"I swear! I was right there at the truck, looking all in the mothafucka; on both sides. That nigga, Snag is lying like a mothafucka!" she exclaimed. "There's no way in the fuck I would've got you out yo sleep, baby, if the nigga was in there." Asia shook her head.

"Don't stress it, sis. It's cool," Ty-Ty said.

"Nooo, bra. Think about it. Why the fuck did Snag just lie? It's a reason. He's hiding something. It's common fucking sense." She sucked her teeth.

"What you thank he hiding, bae?" Smoke asked.

She looked out the window. "Man, I don't know." She poked her lip out.

A few hours later, Asia called J-Bo. He told her to come see him at the Gold's Gym on Austell Road, in Austell, Georgia.

Damn, she thought, looking at J-Bo's chest popping through his shirt. She could see his six pack through the black exercise thermal. His waves were wet with sweat. Asia bit the inside of her lip. *I never knew this nigga looked like this*, she thought.

"What's up, J-Bo?" Asia greeted. She stepped in while going for a hug.

"I'm all sweaty." J-Bo fanned the hug off he seen coming. "What's up?" He walked over to the dumbbells, picking up a thirty pounder in each hand. He looked in her eyes for a hot second before curling his arms, one at a time. She replayed the night before events for him.

"Say what?" he said taking a deep breath. He dropped the dumbbells and went to the treadmill. He set it on low where he could power walk. "So, you saying, he wasn't there, but when you came back he was there, then told you he never left?"

"Yes," she said. "Something just ain't right about that, J-Bo. I got a really bad feeling about it like, my nigga, why did you lie is all I'm saying?"

"But what typa proof you got dat he's lying?" J-Bo asked, turning the speed up on the treadmill.

"Huh?" she asked.

"I'm saying." He ran faster. "What did he say?"

"His lying ass said he was there the whole time." She leaned against one of the treadmills.

"So, in a situation like this, if this was life or death, how would I know who's lyin'?" he asked, slowing down. Asia just stood there looking.

"Always be mindful. Whenever you call somebody a liar; you should be ready to prove it. So, I don't put it past Snag, but still." He slid under the bench press. "What you think he was doin'?" J-Bo asked, pressing 250 pounds.

Asia shrugged her shoulders. "I don't know, bra. It just rubbed me the wrong way by him lying to my face. Smoke's face has gotten better, now. Can he be my security from now on?" she whined.

Finished pressing, J-Bo stood up and sipped from the water bottle that was on the floor. "Naw, shawty. If you thank shawty up to sum funny, I need you close to him. That way we can figure it on out," he said, dropping to do some push-ups. "But, I tell you what," J-Bo said leaping to his feet. "I'll get to the bottom of it today, okay." He faced her. She nodded. "Oh yeah, I meant to tell you the otha day. I'm proud of you." He smiled hard. "The way you was runnin' when y'all thought I was Tez." He chuckled in between deep breaths. "That shit was impressive."

"Thanks," she half-ass said.

***

Later that day, Ty-Ty and J-Bo sat in the living room of J-Bo's already furnished condo in downtown Atlanta. The off blue couch cushions and the orange backs of the chairs matched perfectly with the African type of look he was aiming for. A seventy-two-inch flat screen hung from the wall and on the small glass table was a bottle of Ace of Spades. J-Bo poured him and Ty-Ty a glass, while telling Ty-Ty everything Asia told him.

"What you thinkin', boss?" Ty-Ty asked, sipping the champagne.

J-Bo took a deep breath. "The only reason I even give a fuck is because what happened last night, is something that happened while in da process of findin' Tez and Nae." He sipped his glass. "So, it's on some shit like, what if one of them is protectin' Tez and Nae, and dats how da misunderstandin' between Asia and Snag coming up." He looked at Ty-Ty, trying to read his eyes.

"You know Snag is a big freaky-ass trick. I wouldn't be surprised if he know a prostitute in that neighborhood and ducked off to get some," Ty-Ty added. They both laughed.

"Shit so sad, but crazy, because we know it's true. But I know what I'ma do." J-Bo finished off his glass. "You know where that hoe shop at?" J-Bo stood up.

"What shop?" Ty-Ty asked, finishing his cup.

"The salon on Austell Road," J-Bo reminded.

"Ohh yeah," he remembered. "I know where that shit at."

"I need you there. Just post up. Hit my line if the fat bitch leave," he said walking into his bedroom area.

"What's the plan?" Ty-Ty asked, standing up.

"Can't tell you, cuz. Ion want you to be a suspect." J-Bo smiled.

***

They rode down the street in silence. They had just went to one of the spots to pick up some money, and fill them back up on product. J-Bo was allowing Asia to do it all, so she knows exactly what she's supposed to be doing, and what she will be doing as soon as this Tez and Nae situation is under control.

"No disrespect, bra. But, if you showing Asia her duties, why we gotta be here too?" Smoke asked from the backseat. Snag nodded, agreeing with Smoke.

"Y'all gotta be here because we gotta situation on our hands. Might not be nothin', Might be somethin'," he said, pulling up to their spot in Pittsburgh.

"Same thang. Go in there. Get the money. Make sure it's a number on it and give them this." He handed her the last small brown bag, containing a couple bricks. She got out.

"One of y'all lyin'." J-Bo lit a cigarette.

"Who?" Snag asked quickly.

"That owl, nigga. You or Asia. Somebody lyin'. I don't know why dis is somethin' a nigga would lie about, but it might be somethin', so dis how we gone play it." J-Bo paused, as Asia approached the car. She got in and gave J-Bo a thumbs up. The spot under the seat was already open. She stuffed the small grocery bag of money into it.

"Like I was sayin', Asia is either lyin' about Snag not being in dat car." He inhaled the tobacco, and exhaled a cloud of smoke. "Or Snag is lyin' about not leavin' dat car. Makes me wonder either way. So what we finna do is run in that salon and kill everything movin'. Smoke you stand down. Only shooters I want is Asia and Snag."

Silence. J-Bo looked at Asia. She broke eye contact. He looked at Snag through the rearview. Snag broke eye contact. He looked at Smoke.

"I'll run in there. Let me and Snag do it," Smoke said, trying to spare Asia from putting in the dirty work.

"Nah, I want Asia and Snag. Dats final!" His voice slapped off the glass and into everybody's ears. He turned the music all the way up and rode silently. J-Bo occasionally looked at all three of them during the ride. All of their heads were down, tuned into their phones. *I'm finna get to the bottom of it*, J-Bo thought.

Once at the safe house everybody had to take a leak. J-Bo told Snag to show Asia exactly what to do with the money that she brings there. The two of them went upstairs.

Smell like a damn woodshop up here, Asia thought. A thick wooden table sat in the middle of the floor with two money counting machines on top. There was a black sectional couch with a few shotguns on it and that was it.

"Why the fuck are you lying?" Asia whispered aggressively.

"I'm not fuckin lyin', I swear to God I was in dat damn truck da whole time." His aggressive whispering energy met hers.

Asia shook her head as Snag showed her how to work the money machine and what to do when it jams up. She stared at the digital machine but wasn't paying it any attention at all.

Am I tripping? I think Snag was in that damn truck the first time I went. Why the fuck would he lie about some shit like that? Hell naw, Asia, you not fucking tripping. That lying ass nigga was not in that fucking truck. And as soon as I can prove it, I'ma put his ass in violation, she thought.

"Come on. Let's ride!" J-Bo yelled, coming from the basement with a few ski masks in his hand. In his other hand was a long roller. He was rubbing at his all-black Gucci sweater. He handed them each a mask and he kept one for himself. He rolled the mask on his head.

Back in the car, he put the engine in reverse, backed out and started riding up the street.

"No time for games, or none of that shit," J-Bo said, staring at the road. "Get in there and drop everythang moving." He checked his rearview. "If anythang seems too strange, me and Smoke comin' in behind y'all."

"J-Bo," Snag said, followed by a hard swallow.

"What's up?"

"Bruh, I- just…" he stammered over his words.

"What, nigga?" J-Bo looked at him through the rearview.

"I think a move like dis will keep us farther away from Tez and Nae. Because if we go kill everything moving, Nae's gonna hear about it. And that's probably gonna keep shawty as far away from us as possible," he explained.

J-Bo nodded. "Yea, I undastand, bra. But like I said, kill everything movin." J-Bo was firm.

***

Ty-Ty had been sitting in the truck for hours parked outside of Nae's shop. He got out to stretch his legs. He didn't want to look suspicious with all the black he had on his big body frame, so he went into the Dollar General. He just walked the aisles aimlessly until he eventually purchased some snacks. As he walked out, sipping his fruit punch Powerade, the big girl was outside of the salon. She was looking around very frantically. She dropped the keys twice trying to lock the doors. Ty-Ty turned his head quickly so she wouldn't see him looking at her. She jogged to her small car, almost opening the driver side door and ducking in at the same time she reached it. Cranking up the car, she backed out and sped off. Ty-Ty rushed back to the truck and called J-Bo.

***

"What about cameras? It might be some outside that strip plaza and inside that salon. Come on big bra. You not thanking," said Smoke.

J-Bo laughed. "Cameras? Nigga why the fuck you think I gave y'all masks," J-Bo snapped.

"Okay, what about the license plate? If it's cameras, they gone see that, and this shit gone lead back to whoever name these trucks in," Smoke countered. J-Bo was silent.

"And to be all the way honest, boss. I don't see what killin' everybody in the shop is gone prove," said Smoke.

"It'll prove a lot," J-Bo answered.

"So, you not worried about the plate being seen?" Smoke asked.

"No," J-Bo said calmly. His phone rung. He answered and listened for a few seconds. "Okay, meet me in Pittsburgh." He hung up and turned around at the first light.

"Everythang okay?" Smoke asked because of how fast J-Bo had begun driving.

"Yea, some shit I gotta address. Dis salon shit gotta happen on anotha day. I'll let y'all know when," he said. He pulled up to their small blue house on Smith Street. He reached under the seat for a gun.

"Need one of us witchu?" Snag asked.

"Naw, I got it. I'll tap in later." He tucked the gun and walked towards the house. Asia took the wheel.

***

Ty-Ty pulled up to the house a few moments after Asia pulled off. He greeted the couple young niggas he passed to get into the backroom. J-Bo was pacing the floor.

"What's up, boss?" Ty-Ty asked, clearly seeing frustrations on J-Bo's face.

"One of them mothafuckas is lookin out for Tez and Nae. I believe it now." He closed his fist and swung at the air.

Ty-Ty sat on the barstool, the only piece of furniture in the room. "How you figure that?"

"Ty-Ty, how did you say the bitch left?" he asked sarcastically.

"She was rushing, fam. Kept looking around like a mothafucka was tryna kill her or somethin'."

"Exactly. I told them that we was on our way to the shop, and I wanted Snag and Asia to run in and kill everythang movin'. I wasn't finna let them do dat. I was just tryna see who was gone have the most issue. Then next thing I fuckin' know, da bitch come rushin' out, locking da place up. It ain't nowhere near closin' time. That's why I wanted you there."

"So, one of them hit the big bitch up and told her to get out of there?" Ty-Ty guessed.

J-Bo nodded. "That's the only thang make sense. That's why I wanted you there. I wasn't serious about hurtin' the girl. I just wanted to see something."

"Yea, dat shit make sense." Ty-Ty scratched his graying beard. "That's what you meant by you ain't want me to be a suspect," Ty-Ty realized.

"Yea, I know you solid, bra," J-Bo said, looking in Ty-Ty's eyes. "But in a situation like this, any and everybody is questionable. And I didn't want you in dat category. Dats why ain een tell you what I was gonna do."

"So, what's next? You got to get with Ken?" Ty-Ty asked.

"Not necessarily. It's still shit I can do before I have to bring big bra in it," J-Bo said.

"Well, back in my days, when you got a few suspects, and one situation, and somebody has to be responsible, you know how we handled it?" Ty-Ty asked, standing up stretching.

J-Bo smiled. "Yea, I know," he said, pacing back to the other side of the floor.

"How?" Ty-Ty asked, wanting to be sure. When J-Bo walked back towards him, Ty-Ty threw his arm out and gave him dap. "You said you know how. So in a situation like this, back in the day, how would we have handled it?"

J-Bo nodded. "Kill em all, and you got ya man."

CHAPTER 8

"That's weird," Smoke said, as Asia pulled away from the Pittsburgh trap. He gently rubbed Asia's tense shoulders. "It's gone be aiight, bae." He felt her shoulder muscles harden from stress. She took a deep breath. She moved her upper body according to how good the one handed massage felt. Smoke grinned at her movements.

"What was that about?" she moaned.

"What?" Smoke asked, tightening his massage.

"How the hell J-Bo just jumped out the car talking about he has something to do. But he was just so determined on getting everything that moves killed in the salon."

"Big bruh, be movin' funny sometimes. He don't always tell a nigga what he got going on," Snag chimed in from the back seat.

Asia rolled her eyes. "You're a liar, I don't want to talk to you," Asia calmly said. "Matter fact, where I'm dropping you off at?" she asked.

Snag told her to drop him off at a Young Boss safe house in Riverdale, and she shot to Clayton County with the quickness, letting him out right out front before pulling off.

"That's cool and dandy, miss grown boss," Smoke said seductively, after Snag had gotten out of the truck. "But, for future references," he leaned closer to her. "If a nigga is a liar, stop tellin' them. Play dumb, like you don't know, then catch em red handed." He kissed her lips.

***

"This what I wanna do, Ty-Ty." J-Bo held a finger to his temple. "I want everybody to take a day off. Okay? Everybody amongst us that's on this mission. Everybody gets a day off."

"Aiight, you want me to call it?" Ty-Ty asked, pulling his phone from his pocket.

"Naw, I'm not done. I want somebody trailing Snag, and somebody trailing Asia. Matter fact, two people on Asia, just in case her and Smoke split up. I want eyes on them because I know something is up." He started pacing the floor again, twirling his hands together.

"Ty-Ty, do you realize that it's clear one of these mothafuckas got somethin funny goin on. So once I crack it, then kill Nae and Tez in front of big bro." J-Bo slowly shook his head, holding an evil smile on his face. "He gone leave dis Young Boss shit to me."

"Shid, it's basically yours now," said Ty-Ty.

Ty-Ty waited until the young boys he sent out to do the following called and said they were close to the targets. Then he called and told them J-Bo was proud of everybody for working so hard lately, and he was permitting today to be a day off for them all. He told them don't conduct any Young Boss business. Just strictly enjoy themselves.

Ty-Ty drove. He and J-Bo were quiet. They listened to music the entire ride. J-Bo considered using a GPS to get him to the written down address, but Ty-Ty knew the city well enough to know exactly where he was going. Ty-Ty turned into a complex of opulent houses, right off Clay Road. Unable to stand the idea of being with Shakeena in a house she shared with another man, he had move them from the house on Anderson Mill Road.

"Why the fuck is it so many damn speed bumps in dis neighborhood?" J-Bo asked from the passenger seat. He was frustrated after going over the third speed bump, and there was clearly more to go.

"This a school zone, bro," Ty-Ty answered.

"That's a damn high school across the street."

"Don't matter. School zone is a school zone." Ty-Ty crossed another one as he neared a dead end. "Which house?"

"160," J-Bo said.

"There it go," Ty-Ty said, maneuvering into the open driveway.

J-Bo got out the truck and stretched, still standing in the door way.

"I'm comin' in, boss?" Ty-Ty asked.

"Uhh." J-Bo smiled looking at the big house. There was a three car garage, pretty sunflowers growing in the flower bed, a nicely manicured yard, and fresh rocks outlining the single tree growing on the lawn. J-Bo looked through the small garage windows. He walked back to Ty-Ty.

"Nah, I think I'm straight for now," he said, looking down the street, admiring the neighborhood. He untucked his pistol and handed it to Ty-Ty. "If I call you, come runnin'," he smiled.

J-Bo pulled his key out, unlocked the door and entered. Walking through the house he found Shakeena in the kitchen cooking. He walked up behind her, grabbed a handful of that ass and kissed her on the neck.

"Mmmm." She smiled. "Hey, handsome."

"W'sup. What you cookin'?"

Shakeena stirred a mixed vegetables in a skillet. "Stir fry and rice." There was a pot of rice boiling in a pot in the top right corner of the stove.

"Mhmm. Smells good." J-Bo kissed her neck again. "Where my son at?"

"At my mama house. I don't like him here with it looking like this." She threw her hands up at the empty space of a house she had.

J-Bo stepped back and looked around. "What happened?"

She sucked her teeth and crossed her arms. "Really?" She stared at him.

"What?" He seemed clueless.

"You sent Ken, to take everything, J-Bo," she said, shamefully, dropping her head. "I appreciate you movin' us and all, but this place is just as empty."

"Oh, yea," J-Bo walked over to the barstool area. "Got anythang to drank, shawty?"

She got a plastic cup from the dish washer and pulled some cheap vodka from the fridge, pouring him a drink.

"So, what was the fuckin' point in sendin' my son to, Florida,?" he questioned, downing the shot.

She leaned forward, planting her face into her folded arms on the countertop. J-Bo looked around the house again. He walked around the counter and placed his hand on her back.

"Talk to me," he said, his tone more gentle this time.

"J-Bo, I just didn't—"

"Hold yo fuckin' head up and talk to me, shawty." His voice was aggressive, but not hostile.

"J-Bo, I just don't want my...—our son in this house like this," she cried, wiping her face. "Everyday he's asking about a TV; where's the couch? Where's my bed..."

"Ken took his shit?" J-Bo clenched his teeth.

"No, he didn't touch anything in his room." She leaped up to sit on the counter.

I was finna say, J-Bo thought. "You need to call yo mama and let her know JJ is coming back home. Go get dressed." He frowned at the pajamas she had on.

"J-Bo, I literally don't have any clothes here. Ken took everything," she sobbed.

"And how fuckin' long ago has dat shit been, shawty? Weeks to a month!" he snapped. "You mean to tell me you been sittin' on yo ass not doin' shit! You ain't went and got no typa money to put a new outfit on yo fuckin' back?" He slammed a fist on the counter, and poured himself another shot.

Shakeena dropped her head when he silently stared at her with that fire in his eyes.

"Go take a fuckin shower! Hurry up," he said walking from the kitchen, out the house and hopping back in the passenger side of the truck. Ty-Ty got in on the driver side. "You good, boss?"

"Yea," J-Bo said. "I'm good."

But he wasn't. He had forgiven Shakeena, but it was hard to forget. There were times where he loved and and that loved shined through, and there were moments when he hated her and felt pure rage towards her for what having their son believing he was dead and that another man was his father. An O.G in prison had once told him that broken things can become blessed things if you let God do the mending. He was just hoping there was some truth to that.

"Keenaa!" he hollered from the passenger window, towards the house. She came speed walking out a few seconds later and got in the backseat.

J-Bo told Ty-Ty to stop by one of the new East Atlanta safe houses he set up when he first out, and they pulled up. He went inside and took fifty grand out of the million in cash Ken gave him as a welcome home present. They went to Saks Fifth Avenue in Atlanta, and J-Bo bought her a pair of black Christian Louboutin red sole pumps, a pair of Rag & Bone blue jeans, and an all-white Jimmy Choo hoodie. He paid for it, then told Shakeena to go in a dressing room and change into it. He purchased himself and Ty-Ty each an all-white sweatshirt with the word *Dior* spelled out in bold, black street styled letters.

Next, they went to a luxury hairdresser in Southwest Atlanta. He paid for Shakeena's natural long black hair to be washed and done however she wanted. He stayed in the car with Ty-Ty, while she was inside getting it done.

"Bitch got da nerve to be out here lookin lika whole fuckin' crackhead, fam," he said lighting a cigarette.

Ty-Ty chuckled. "Shiiid, you stripped her of everything."

"But still, you don't get up and go get nothin'? I can easily say fuck dis hoe, take my son, and leave her down bad." He took a hard pull, blew it out and took another one.

"She know good hearted J-Bo ain't gone do her like that," Ty-Ty laughed.

J-Bo smiled. "Yea, wateva, nigga." He exhaled. "What's up with Asia nem? I wanna find out who our traitor is." He pulled on the Newport short again, then flicked the filter out the window. Ty-Ty hit a few numbers on his phone and made a few calls.

"Fam say Asia and Smoke went to dinner. Been back in the house every since. Say Snag, been on Fulton Industrial." They both laughed.

"Now what da fuck is on Fulton Industrial Boulevard except for dem stankin' pussy forty dolla hoes?" J-Bo asked, still laughing.

"Much as that nigga trick off, we might need to send some hoes at him. Get rich quick," Ty-Ty added. Just as they were laughing again, Shakeena came walking to the truck.

"What?" she smiled once J-Bo rolled the window down.

"You look different. You got it pressed?"

"My real hair was breaking so bad, and uneven so she cut it short, and put in a full lace wig. This hair..." She fingered through it. It stopped at the top of her butt. "...is Brazilian."

"How much?" J-Bo asked, pulling another cigarette from the pack.

"Eight hundred," she mumbled.

"I see why Snag be settling for the forty dolla deals," Ty-Ty joked.

J-Bo chuckled and handed her a thousand. "Tip her."

Lastly, they went to a furniture store in Lithia Springs called Perfect Dreamer. He bought her a white and tan king sized five-piece bedroom set, an all-white-five-piece dining room set, a tan leather sofa, a matching love seat, and a few seventy-two-inch flat screen TV's. They said they would deliver it all the next day.

"I appreciate you, Jerome," she said as they walked in the house.

"I'ma be out here, boss," Ty-Ty said, standing in the porch.

J-Bo nodded and closed the door. "So, what you gone do?"

"Do about what?"

"About yo fuckin' life, Keena. Like, Ion get how you really ain't been doin' shit, shawty."

She whipped her bob styled hair to the side. "J-Bo, you've had me spoiled. I haven't had to do shit in the past what… twelve years or so years? J-Bo, I never thought about doing shit. And one day, it all gets taken away from me." Her eyes watered.

"Don't fuckin cry, shawty. You dead wrong." His words held pain.

"I know, baby," she whispered, as the tears begin falling again. "I'm so sorry, J-Bo. I thought you were gone forever. I was just trying to maintain a life that I was used to."

He snatched away from her. "That's a fuckin lie! You know money ain't neva been a fuckin issue! You could've still had dat same fuckin luxury life!" he barked in her face.

"But I want physicality too, Jerome!" Her yell quickly turned into a weak cry.

He grabbed her and held her tight. Once she stopped crying he squeezed her butt. She turned around and started twerking on him. She dropped to her knees when she felt his dick stiffen. She took the first button on his pants loose. He took off his shirt and sweater.

"You been working out daddy," she moaned, sliding her tongue across his six pack. She undid the other two buttons and pulled his soft dick out. She looked up at him in his eyes, stroking him slowly so he could fully harden, and ran her other hands through his thick pubic hairs. "You had any since you been out?" she asked seductively. He shook his head. She took him into her mouth. She squeezed his butt cheeks, pushing him into her face as she sucked with an almost animalistic enthusiasm. His knees started buckling quick. He pulled out of her mouth and got on his knees with her. Already knowing what time it was, she quickly took her pants off and got on all fours. Her juicy ass cheeks spread open. He fucked her hard, pulling her hair, calling her all kinds of stupid bitches. Three minutes later he was pulling out shooting thick white cum. They laid on the floor, exhausted.

"Get dat shit off me," he said between deep breaths. She leaned over and licked and sucked all the semen up. She showed it to him on her tongue before swallowing it.

"I'ma get it together, J-Bo."

"What you wanna do with yo life, shawty?" He used his t-shirt to dry himself then pulled his pants up.

"I think I want to do hair." She cocked her head to the side.

"So, you need to look up a class so you can learn how to do it."

"Well, this girl Kimberly, she work at that shop Nae had opened up not too long ago in Austell. She been trying to get me to come help her there for like the past week. I just haven't went. She said she'll teach me how to do hair, and she said when I get the hang of it I can make like a thousand a week." Excitement bounced off her words.

"Wait, wait, wait," J-Bo said, sitting up. "Who you just said?" He frowned.

"Her name is Kimberly. She's a hairdresser."

"Nah, you said sum about, Nae, didn't you?" he questioned.

"Yea, she works for Nae at that hair salon," she reiterated.

"In Austell?" J-Bo searched his memory.

"Yes."

"Call her! Tell her you wanna help." His eyes bolted big.

"Okay, I will. But why you say it like that?" she frowned.

"I need this right now, baby. I need to find Nae, asap!" He jumped to his feet smiling. "Man, you need to get in good with that girl and find out where Nae at!"

Chapter 9

"Nigga, tell me why a bitch dat works for Nae been callin, tryna get Keena to come help her out at the salon," J-Bo said excitedly, stepping on the front porch.

Ty-Ty smiled, rubbing his hands together. "What?Hell yea! We about to get paid!" His excitement was equivalent to J-Bo's.

"Hell yea, nigga!" J-Bo gave Ty-Ty a hug like a happy kid would do. "Fam, we gone handle they ass and get dat two M's. Long as Asia nem ain't tied to them, we gone break dem off like…" He looked up in thought. "Fifty racks apiece!"

"And if we find out they are, we just going to split the two M's, and and knock off whoever involved," Ty-Ty added.

"You already know," J-Bo said, giving Ty-Ty dap. "I'm finna make her get on top of dat now. So I'ma kick it in here for a minute. You can slide off if you need to do sum."

Ty-Ty shook his head. "Naw, boss. I'm security. I be damned if I leave any opportunity for something to happen to you. I'm straight out here."

"Ok," J-Bo smiled, going back in the house."Is Kimberly a fat bitch?" J-Bo asked, walking up to Shakeena. She was still on the floor in the same spot.

She laughed. "You're so disrespectful boy."

"Man fuck all dat! Is she?" He sat down next to her.

"She's a plus sized beautiful woman," she answered.

"When you plannin' on callin'?"

"You want me to call now?" she asked.

"Yea."

Shakeena made the call. Kimberly told her it's a lot of shit going on, right now. Therefore, she shut the shop down until further notice. She told Shakeena she would give her a call as soon as she got the issue taken care of. J-Bo laid on his back, locking his fingers behind his head. Shakeena rested her head against his chest. J-Bo closed his eyes. . .

"Hold up, man! Dat damn couch cost racks! Be careful with it, scraping da damn door!" J-Bo snapped on the furniture movers as they struggled carrying the expensive leather couch.

"Racks?" the young, skinny, white boy asked, as they sat the couch an inch away from the wall as Shakeena instructed.

"What?" J-Bo frowned.

"You said racks? I'm not familiar with that term, sir." His voice was soft like a kitten.

"Racks, nigga. Thousands of dollars." J-Bo dug in his pocket and counted out four thousand dollars. "Racks!"

"Come on, bro," the other young, white boy, a little bigger in size said, pulling at his co-workers shirt. They walked out the door to get more furniture.

"Prison made somebody mean as hell," Shakeena joked.

Naw, shawty." J-Bo half smiled.

"You have a really nice smile, Jerome." She stared at his teeth.

"Preciate it," he mumbled.

As they moved the rest of the furniture in, J-Bo was silently sitting on the couch, on his phone. He downloaded a few social media apps and started creating accounts. Shakeena escorted the two young workers through the house showing them where she wanted each piece of furniture.

Multiple hours later. . .

"Tip them," she whispered to J-Bo, after the two young men had loaded all the furniture, mounted all the TVs, and put her bedroom set together. They were exiting the house, exhausted.

"Please," she begged. J-Bo gave her four hundred dollars. She gave the boys two hundred each.

"Racks," the smaller boy joked, gratefully pocketing the two bills.

J-Bo couldn't help but to let out a slight laugh. He closed his eyes and stretched, rubbing his eyelids. Staring at the glare from his phone's screen for so long caused a minor blur in his vision.

"Now it kinda feels like home," he said, looking around the now full living room. He went into the dining room, then into the kitchen. He opened the cabinets and refrigerator. They were empty.

"What you been eatin, shawty?" he asked, when Shakeena entered the kitchen behind him.

"I been ordering out."

"How much money you got left?"

She dropped her head. "Twenty dollars," she answered, embarrassed.

He pulled the four grand from his pocket and gave it to her before going upstairs.

Dis shit fye, J-Bo thought, entering the bedroom. The big bed took up a third of the room. The two dressers, one of which had a long and wide mirror connected, and the nightstand, filled the room perfectly.

"Smell like fresh wood," J-Bo said inhaling deeply. He kicked his shoes off and stepped onto the big tan rug, laid out before the bed. Shakeena was right beside him.

"Oh my God, it feels like cotton," she said.

J-Bo smiled then crawled into the bed, laying on his back. She hopped in next, scooting close to him. He closed his eyes again.

"I love you, J-Bo," she whispered.

He opened his eyes just enough to lock eyes with her. "Yea, I love you too, shawty." He closed his eyes and she slowly unbuttoned his pants. He lifted up his bottom when he felt her tugging at his jeans. She pulled his pants down to his thighs, then started massaging her face against his flaccid dick through his boxers. She kissed and licked the cotton fabric, making his dick jump.

Again, he lifted his bottom at the feel of her pulling on his boxers. The second his underwear went past his dick she grabbed it and took him into her mouth. It was halfway hard as she pushed her face all the way into his pelvic area. That made him harden fully, and she didn't budge to move back. J-Bo scooted back. She pulled his eight inches from the back of her throat and started stroking it slow.

"I love how this chocolate dick look," she moaned, before she started sucking the tip while stroking his shaft. Thick saliva ran down her knuckles.

"Aww, shit!" J-Bo released a deep moan.

"Don't run from me, Jerome," she whispered, taking him all the way into her mouth again. She repeated that three times then went down to his big hairy balls. She licked and slurped on them, whole time stroking his dick. He opened his eyes.

"Ahh, you nasty, bitch," he moaned, digging his head into the pillows.

She went a bit lower than his balls and licked that space in between his butt and nuts. He scooted back and she scooted forward, not moving her face. He pushed her forehead, but she didn't move.

"Ahh, I'm finna cum," he moaned.

She started deep throating him until she felt his dick flinching. She then stroked him fast, flicking her tongue all around his tip.

"Fuck!" he moaned.

As the thick creamy semen shot out of him, she treated his dick like lipstick, sliding him all over her lips. Some of his sperm dropped off her chin. She swallowed the majority of it. J-Bo looked at her after she released his now marshmallow soft organ. She started flicking her tongue at him. He shook his head before dropping it into the pillows again.

"You heard something?" she asked, looking back.

Without looking up, he shook his head no. She wiped her mouth and headed out the room.

I need to let his lil security guard know right now not to just be walking in my house whenever he damn feel like it, she thought.

Reaching the top of the steps she heard movement. The front door was open.

This nigga just all through my shit, and gone have the nerve to leave the fucking door open, she thought.

Halfway down the steps, she saw two people standing in the living room whispering. They were dressed in all black and were both masked. One of the people was wiping their gloved hands off on the couch, leaving a dark brownish red color stain. One of the men saw her. She ran back up the steps. He ran behind her. Looking back once at the top of the stairs, she didn't see anybody. She ran into the bedroom.

"J-Bo! J-Bo!" She screamed hysterically, jumping into the bed.

"What's up?" He jumped up quick, looking around, scanning the room.

"Somebody's in the house!" She clutched a pillow.

"It ain't nobody but Ty-Ty. Dat's the bro." He looked down at the wet mess in his lap.

"No, J-Bo!" She looked at the door and back to him. "It's two niggas. They got on masks. One of them just chased me!" she cried.

"What da fuck!" He jumped up and pulled up his pants, securing the buttons. He snatched Shakeena by the wrist, slung her into the large walk-in closet, and took off out the room. In the hallway he walked slow, giving all of his attention to each door.

Why da fuck did I leave my strap in da truck with Ty-Ty. Ain't no way Ty-Ty let two niggas run in on me. He must be down wit' Asia nem, tryna get me out da way, he thought as he busted through the bathroom door in the hallway. It was clear. Then JJ's room. Clear. The guest room and bathroom were also clear. At the top of the steps he could see the front door was wide open. He took a deep breath before running down the steps. He looked to the left while heading down, but didn't see anybody. He saw the stain on the couch and instantly knew it was blood. He ran full speed out the front door.

What da fuck time is it? he wondered, seeing the sky was dark.

Ty-Ty was sitting in the truck behind the wheel.

Oh, you was down with these niggas, he thought, walking furiously towards the driver's side. He snatched the door open.

"Nigga, you…" His words were cut off when he saw the deep gash on the side of Ty-Ty's neck, leaving veins hanging out. He reached over Ty-Ty and hit the button on the volume knob. He reached under the seat but there was nothing there. He turned his head, not able to stomach Ty-Ty sitting there lifeless as he patted his waistline. He felt the metal and snatched it from Ty-Ty's hip. He instantly threw up after looking at Ty-Ty again. He ran back into the house with the gun trained chest high, ready to shoot anybody that wasn't Shakeena.

His index finger was almost pulling at the trigger as he ran in and cleared the living room. He then cleared the dining room, kitchen, and the garage. It was all clear. He leaped up the steps, two at a time, checking JJ's room, the guest room, and the bathroom again. It was clear.

The bedroom door was closed. He kicked under the knob. The door broke and slung open. Shakeena was lying on her stomach on the bed, with a knot of blanket stuffed in her mouth. One of the masked people stood over her. One hand was full of her hair twisted up. The other hand held a sharp hunters knife to her neck. The other intruder stood in the center of the floor with a gun aimed at him.

The man pulled off his mask. "Put da gun down J-Bo," Tez said.

"Get dat fuckin knife off her fuckin neck!" he barked, keeping his aim right between Tez's eyes.

"Baby, if I have to tell him again, cut dat bitch throat," Tez said.

"Okay, daddy," the masked woman responded.

"Nae," J-Bo said angrily, recognizing her voice immediately.

"J-Bo," Tez said, calmly grinning.

"I'm not dropping my gun, Martez. You know dis!"

Tez looked at Nae and nodded. J-Bo dropped to the ground and let off two shots, sending Tez down. By the time he turned his aim towards Nae, she had already started cutting Shakeena's neck.

"J-Bo!" Shakeena winced in pain. He sent three shots to Nae.

"J-Bo!" Shakeena's yell turned into a faint whisper.

"J-Bo," Shakeena said.

J-Bo jumped up from the floor to his feet. He was covered in sweat bullets, breathing deep and rapidly as if he was being held under water. His eyes were wide as saucers. Shakeena stood up.

"You alright, shawty?" he asked, looking around the room.

"I'm okay, baby. You scared me. You were breathing and sweating so hard."

"Where's da furniture?"

"Remember they said they not bringing it until tomorrow, baby," she reminded him.

He took off for the front door, snatching it open and looking at the sky, it was dark.

Shit, he thought, running towards the truck. He saw Ty-Ty's body behind the driver's seat. He snatched the door open and met face to face with the barrel of Ty-Ty's Glock 9.

"My bad boss." Ty-Ty lowered the weapon. "You good?"

J-Bo let out an overdue exhale. "Yea, I had a fucked up dream. Come on, let's go."

CHAPTER 10

"Damn, fam! You was tripping hard like that?" Ty-Ty asked, as he drove through the night.

"Hell yea, nigga," J-Bo replied, placing an open palm over the left side of his chest. "Bra, I can still feel my heart beatin' like a mothafucka. That shit felt real as fuck."

Ty-Ty shook his head. "I don't like that type of shit, fam. Talkin' bout' my neck was cut open." He clenched his jaws.

"Shiiid, I already know. We gotta find dis bitch ass nigga!" J-Bo looked out the window then back to Ty-Ty. "Matter fact, tap in with the guys about Asia nem."

"Already did. That's why I didn't see you walkin' up on the truck. Nigga when that door opened, I was bout to blow that bitch." Ty-Ty smiled.

"I know you was. You up'd dat pistol quick, fam. Dat's good doe. Dat mean you on point."

Ty-Ty shook his head. "No, J-Bo. Don't try to make it sound like that, bro. I was slippin' and you know I was." Ty-Ty beat himself up about it.

"How da hell was you slippin', fam?" J-Bo asked.

"Because, if you were somebody different, a real threat, I could've been dead without that door ever openin'. Then that gives a nigga opportunity to run in the house and hurt you and Keena. That shit will never happen again."

"Ty-Ty, bra, you gotta care about yoself before others, my nigga. I know you take security serious and I appreciate you for that. But damn fam, you act like you got more love for Young Boss, than you do for yo damn self," J-Bo said.

"I do."

"Do you love yoself, bro?" J-Bo asked.

Silence.

J-Bo looked out the window, shaking his head. "Anyway, what the young boys say?"

"Asia and Smoke went to Ruth's Chris Steak House, then back home. But your boy Snag, on the other hand…" He paused to make a turn.

J-Bo turned towards Ty-Ty, laying on him to give some info.

"They say he was on Delk Road in Marietta at the Day's Inn hotel for a hot little minute."

J-Bo sat back, fanning his hand. "Oh, shiiid, we already know why he was there." J-Bo shook his head. "I wonder why da fuck dat nigga ain't got dem teeth fixed yet," he laughed.

"I don't know, fam. But that's not the kicker," Ty-Ty said, pulling up to the safe house.

"What you mean?" J-Bo reclined the seat back and fucked around with his phone.

"Say he was in the room for a long time and—"

"Yea, he got money. So long as he payin', da bitch gone let him stay fa long as he want. You know that."

"J-Bo, I got the utmost respect for you, fam. Don't cut me off like that, bro. It's more to it."

"You right, my nigga. My bad. Go head. What you was sayin'?" he said, texting Shakeena.

"They say he was in there for about two hours. So, when he left, bro went to that same room and knocked on the door, acting like he's trying to buy some pussy. But nobody answered. Then one of them twenty dollar selling pussy bitches came from the room next to it and told him that room is empty and tried to get him to come in her room. Say he told her he know a girl in that room because he was there an hour ago. And the girl told him a girl hadn't worked out of that room in days," Ty-Ty explained, digging through his gray beard.

J-Bo frowned. "He sure that's the room Snag came out of?"

"Fam say he a thousand percent positive that's the room he came out of."

"Snag in here," J-Bo asked, nodding towards the safe house.

"Should be."

***

Early the next morning it was back to business. Snag called Asia and told her he was on the way to get the day started. She called J-Bo and asked him could Smoke be her personal security instead of Snag. He declined and told her to just play it cool because he wanted her to be able to pick up on any funny shit he had going on that could possibly lead them to Tez.

"Go to the hospital. I want to check on our chief," Asia said, stepping up into the truck.

Snag nodded his head. "Say less." His voice was groggy.

The ride was silent. The vibe was awkward.

"What?" Asia asked, feeling as if Snag kept looking at her a certain type of way.

"Nothin'," he ensured. "You talked to J-Bo this morning?"

"No. Was I supposed to?"

"Yea. He slept at the safe house last night while I was there. Nigga act like he was scared to go to sleep or sum."

"Why would he be scared to go to sleep at the safe house?" She raised an eyebrow.

Snag shrugged. "Say he just had a nightmare that Tez and Nae had kilt him and his baby mama."

Asia gasped. "Really?"

"Hell yea. That shit too crazy. He want us to find Tez ass bad now."

"Shiiid, I bet he do. Who wouldn't?"

"I'ma find him." He grinned. "I swear I am. I'ma find him and dat bitch."

"How you so sure you're going to be the one to find them?"

"I'm super-duper ambitious. I won't quit." He looked at her then back at the road.

You should've been super-duper ambitious about fixing yo fucking teeth then, she thought, as they entered the hospital's parking lot. They signed in. The nurse had to go ask Flip if he wanted to see them.

"I'm sorry, ma'am. But Mr. Dew said he doesn't want any company."

Asia's face showed bafflement. "Did you tell him who it is?"

"Yes, ma'am, I did. And he don't have to have visitors if he don't want to. So, I'm going to have to ask y'all to leave." She tooted her nose up at Snag.

Back in the car Asia went through her contacts and called Flip's phone. It rung twice then was sent to voicemail. She pressed redial. This time it went straight to voicemail. She called J-Bo. It rung to no avail.

"Where's J-Bo?" she asked.

"What time is it?" Snag asked.

She looked at her phone. "7:10 am."

"He's definitely prolly at that damn gym."

"Get us there," she said, leaning back in her seat closing her eyes.

Snag stepped on it. Before long, they were pulling into Gold Gym parking lot.

Asia stayed in the car. Snag went inside. A few minutes later, Ty-Ty came out the doors of the gym. He had a pair of black tinted glasses on. He looked around the parking lot slowly, before looking back at J-Bo, who stood on the other side of the glass. He gave him a thumbs up and J-Bo came walking out. Snag was right behind him. J-Bo was drenched in sweat. The all black compression suit he wore fitted so tight, you'd think his muscles were about to rip through the fabric. He looked mean as a wet cat.

"What's up?" J-Bo asked, standing at Asia's window.

"I went to visit Flip, and he denied my visit."

J-Bo frowned. "What? Did he know it was you?"

She nodded. "Yes, the nurse said she told him my name and he said he didn't want to see anybody."

"Grab my phone fam," J-Bo said over his shoulder. Ty-Ty went and got his phone from the truck. J-Bo called Flip three times and got no answer.

"Ion know what da fuck typa shit cuz got goin on." J-Bo thought aloud, handing his phone back to Ty-Ty. "He prolly in his feelings bout sum shit. I'll tap in wit him later." He looked back at Snag. "What y'all finna do?"

"Go back to the drawing board, I guess," Asia answered.

He wiped some sweat from his head. "Nah, come here. Ride wit me today."

Asia got out the car.

"She ridin' wit me today, fam," J-Bo told Snag.

Snag nodded, and hopped in the driver seat. He said his farewells, backed out and pulled off.

J-Bo got his shit together, and they loaded up in the truck; Ty-Ty in the driving seat, J-Bo in the passenger seat, and Asia in the back.

"You be getting it in fam," Ty-Ty laughed, pulling away from the gym.

"Hell yea. Got to." J-Bo smiled, flexing his muscles, proud of his physical accomplishments over the years.

"Where to, boss?" asked Ty-Ty.

"Hit da safe house. Let me get a showers," J-Bo answered. "Asia, you know how to shoot?"

Asia shrugged. "Not really."

"You finna learn today," he said.

After J-Bo took a shower, they got back on the road.

"They say it's a good shooting range in Atlanta close…"

"Nah." J-Bo cut her off. "We got our own shootin range, sis."

Ty-Ty laughed, merging onto the highway.

Forty minutes later, they pulled into the driveway of a big traditional ranch styled house in Covington.

"Damn, who house is this?" Asia asked from the backseat, looking at the big three car garage house. The yard was perfectly manicured. "Eww," she said stepping from the truck, turning her nose up. "It smell like shit!"

J-Bo and Ty-Ty laughed.

"Horses," Ty-Ty said, approaching the front door. An older black man opened the door, and they embraced each other and talked for a while.

"Old School. We fuck wit' him. This his farm. He let us lay our shootin' range out here," J-Bo explained.

Ty-Ty walked around the house. J-Bo fanned for her to follow him, and they both followed Ty-Ty. On the right side of the two acres were several horses. On the other side was an open field with a long wooden table closer to the house. There was another wooden table a couple of feet taller than the first. Ty-Ty and J-Bo picked it up and moved it fifteen feet across from the first table. The slim, balding, old man made several trips from the back of the house, loading different guns onto the first table. He then brought two five gallon buckets and placed it in the floor next to the table. He gave a thumbs up to the fellas before going back into the house. There were hundreds of glass soda and juice bottles stacked on crates beside the house.

"Come here." J-Bo called Asia to the first table. Ty-Ty carried one of the sixty bottle crates to the other table and set ten of them up in a row, before coming back to the first table.

"Dis prolly good fa you, shawty," J-Bo said, picking up a gun. "Dis a Kel Tec CP33."

She frowned. "That big ole gun."

"It doesn't really have recoil. It's easy. Look." He grabbed an appropriate magazine from the bucket, slapped it in the gun, and started squeezing the trigger. The shooting startled Asia.

"You betta get used to it." J-Bo handed her the gun. Ty-Ty set up ten more bottles. J-Bo had hit them all. "You got twenty-two moe shots. Hit dem bottles."

It's not that heavy, she thought, raising the gun with one hand. J-Bo grabbed her other hand and positioned it around the butt of the gun.

J-Bo shook his head. "Don't try to do what you seen me do."

She squeezed the trigger and her arms went up. J-Bo stood behind her and wrapped his arms around hers. "Dis gun don't got much kickback. It's ya mind trickin' you, makin' you think it's 'pose to go up high like dat. Just relax, shawty."

Staring at the glass bottle, she squeezed the trigger again.

"Stop shootin' on the side. Aim right at dat bitch, and hit it." J-Bo tightened his grip around her arms and hands. "You could be put in a situation where you make this shot or you and everybody you love dies."

Her jawline got tight, and she pulled the trigger. A big smile covered her face when she hit the glass. J-Bo felt her hands coming loose and kept his firm, making her grip it again.

"He came deep wit' his niggas. Kill em all!" He turned her aim until she shot at all the bottles. When she finished there were four bottles still standing. J-Bo released her.

"Oh my God. I hit them," she exclaimed, jumping in joy. J-Bo stood there looking at her with no type of expression on his face. "What?" she asked.

He pointed to the bottles. "You still got four men alive. One is too many, shawty. So, four is way too many."

She aimed at the bottles and squeezed the trigger until the magazine was empty. Still three bottles standing. She looked at J-Bo. He took the Kel Tec from her and gave her a standard 9mm, the same kind they have in all of their trucks.

"Dat one got a lil more kick to it. So hold it firm. Take sum of dat damn stress off ya shoulders. Think about it like me and Ty-Ty are injured, and we need you to shoot. If you don't hit these three targets, we all gone die," J-Bo said, stepping away from her.

She took aim, and pulled the trigger. *Click! Click!* The gun didn't erupt. She looked at J-Bo.

He smiled. "You see how light dat gun feels?"

She nodded.

"Do da one's we got feel da same way?"

"No, those are a lil heavier," she answered.

"Dat's da exact type gun, shawty." He grabbed a clip out the bucket and put it into the gun. "You need to know the difference between a gun dat's loaded and one dat's not." He handed it back to her. She emptied the clip, flinching at every pull of the trigger. She hit each target.

She smiled. "I got them all."

"Yea, but dat shit took way too much shootin'. We woulda been dead."

J-Bo and Ty-Ty moved the second table a little closer. J-Bo told her to reload the 9. It took her a minute but she eventually got it done. Ty-Ty placed one bottle on the table. J-Bo walked to the back of the house where a bunch of miscellaneous items were and pulled a blanket from the shelf. He unfolded it and spread it out in the center of the field where they stood, about six feet away from the table with the glass on it.

"You're in a situation where a nigga is finna beat you and rape you because you a fine ass yella bone wit a fat ass. After he done raping you, he gone stab you in da neck a million times. He just got butt naked and knocked you to da floor." J-Bo stepped behind her. "Now he's coming at you. You got about three seconds before he starts cuttin' you up. Yo gun on ya side." He took the 9mm from her hand, stretched the belt area of her pants, and stuffed the barrel. "Three seconds and you'll be raped and dead, if he gets to you. He can over power you and take the gun. You gotta hit him in da head, shawty," J-Bo said. Before she could ask a question, he placed both of his hands on the back of her shoulders and used his strength to pull her to the ground.

"Three!" he barked, stepping to the side the second her body had fallen completely.

Asia pulled the 9mm from her hip, deciding how to hold it from the ground angle.

"Two!" J-Bo continued barking.

She raised her arms, getting a perfect aim.

"One!" As he was saying *one*, she was pulling the trigger.

J-Bo smiled at her as he helped her up. Once up he hugged her. "You got em," he said.

Ty-Ty set up ten bottles. J-Bo told Asia to go behind the first table like they were originally.

"We not leavin till you hit all ten," J-Bo said. She started squeezing the trigger. One bottle left standing. "You shootin' to much, shawty." J-Bo fussed as he reloaded the clip. "Dis gun got sixteen shots. You only got ten targets. Hit all dem bottles, and it betta be six shots left in dis gun." He handed the gun back to her.

She focused her aim and pulled the trigger. A few seconds later all the bottles were broken. There were six shots left. J-Bo smiled.

"Yea!" he shouted, hugging her. "Come on, let's ride."

After leaving the range, they headed over to Five Guys. Ty-Ty stood outside the truck and ate. Asia and J-Bo sat in the backseat of the truck and ate their burger and fries.

"You did good," J-Bo said, crunching up a few fries.

"Thank you." She sipped her Sprite. "It was fun."

"I'll take you back soon," he said

"J-Bo, you know the other night." She took a small bite of her burger.

"What other night?" he said between a big bite.

"When me and Snag were outside that girl's house…"

"Yea, what about it?" he asked.

"I really believe Snag was in that girl's house. It just don't makes sense," she frowned. "I promise you. I'm not lying."

J-Bo chewed through his double cheeseburger like a hungry wolf. He used his Mountain Dew to wash the beef down. "I'ma look into it, shawty."

"Okay," she said, dipping a fry in ketchup.

They finished eating. Ty-Ty took the trash inside, then got back behind the wheel. J-Bo called Shakeena.

"Hey, baby, are you okay?" she answered.

"Yea, I'm good. Yo friend, Kimberly, you know about a nigga she fuck wit'?"

"Umm, she used to talk to this dude. I don't remember his name."

"He Young Boss?"

"Yea, I mean, I don't know. He's in some type of gang, though."

"You eva met em?" He scratched his beard.

"Once."

J-Bo sat straight up. "What he look like?"

"Dark brown skin, a little shorter than you, I think." She racked her brain.

"Ugly mothafucka?" He grinned.

Shekeena laughed. "Uhh, yea, he had bad skin."

Oh shit, I know it's Snag, he thought.

"He missin' teeth?" He asked.

"No. He had a nice smile."

CHAPTER 11

Ken stretched out in the big queen sized bed, and looked around the plush Air B&B room they'd rented and smiled. It was fully furnished with glass furniture and the doors were marble. The room was so shiny and peaceful. If you were standing outside looking in, you'd think the whole room was wet. He looked over to his right side. Zaya was still asleep on her stomach. The silk covering had slid off of her lower body. He looked at her charcoal black, slim, long legs for a few seconds; then at her ass. The sides were wrapped with pieces of the light green lace of crotchless lingerie she wore. Her ass was perfectly rounded and poked up just right for her petite body, at least while she was naked. In a pair of jeans you couldn't really tell that she had booty back there.

Ken quietly scooted towards the end of the bed and looked again.

Fuck, he thought, quietly moaning. He slid his hand in his white Jordan shorts, gripping his dick. It started throbbing as he looked at the back of her shaved pussy busting through her thighs. He stroked his shaft slowly, thinking about climbing on top of her, but changed his mind. He covered the rest of her body with the blanket, then went into the bathroom.

How the fuck you wear some panties like that, spend the night with a nigga, and still don't let me fuck, Ken thought, shaking his head. He used an electric toothbrush to brush his teeth. After he finished, he went to the glass dresser, with the big flat screen on top and used the Bob Marley weed grinder to break up a few of the big Zaza buds he'd left there the night before. He ripped apart a Back Woods cigar, dumping the guts in the toilet and rolling it up perfectly. He rolled four grams. The blunt looked like a gorilla's thumb when he finished. He put on his white bath robe that hung from the end of the bed.

He pocketed his phone from the dresser, grabbed the small torch lighter and stepped onto the balcony. He inhaled deeply.

Texas just smells different, he thought, smiling. He lit the blunt and pulled on it hard and slow. Their skyrise Air B&B sat in the middle of Houston. He looked over the city. *I could live here. Shit look different from Atlanta. Women are thicker.*

His phone rung. He instantly recognized the number.

"Good morning," he answered.

"Good morning. Is this Mr. Kenith Griffith?" a young sounding lady asked.

"Yes, it is. How are you?" he asked.

"I'm doing fine today, sir. I'm calling you today for security and verification purposes," she started. "Can you please verify the last four digits of your social security number?"

"Listen, I don't know what the hell is going on, but I've been having to verify a lot of stuff lately. And I don't appreciate you all blocking my debit card the other night until I verified. So, no! I can't verify a damn thing. An if we have this issue again, I promise you, I'm moving all my money to a different bank!" Ken hung up. He took a toke at the blunt and they were calling back. This time it was a man.

"Mr. Griffith, this is Danny, the shift manager…"

"Yea, I know who you are." Ken cut him off with his voice full of smoke.

"Sir, trust me. I understand your frustrations. But it's very urgent that I speak to you about a transaction before processing," he said.

Ken blew a chest full of smoke out. "The rental car, yes. The Air B&B, yes. Thirty thousand dollar withdrawal the other night, yes. I did it," Ken answered, knowing what they wanted already.

"Okay, thank you, sir. And what about the 2.6-million-dollar transaction from this morning?" the man asked.

Ken stopped smoking the blunt in mid pull. "What?" he asked sharply.

"Yes, sir. I see you have several accounts, one of which is a joint account with your wife, Nae Griffith. I see you've made a few transactions for ten thousand dollars each to your joint account with Mrs. Griffith. But I had to call today and just verify with you because of the amount. So, I'm just making sure you are the one making this transaction before I process it."

Ken frowned. "For how much?"

"You attempted to transfer 2.6 million dollars into your joint bank account from your primary checking account."

Ken squeezed the half blunt in his palm, not even feeling the burning end, and threw it over the balcony. "No! I did not do that. Nor have I made any transactions for ten thousand dollars! Why the hell wouldn't you call and verify that, just like you did for today?"

"Well, sir, you don't have a two factor authentication set-up on your account. But the bank automatically does it for any transaction exceeding fifty thousand dollars. I can get with my supervisor who's over the region and see about putting a hold on the bank account that your money was transferred to."

"You said it was transferred into the joint account that I share with my wife."

"Yes, sir. But it was all transferred to a different account since then."

Ken shook his head. "Okay, please set my account so that y'all will contact me if the spending limit exceeds ten thousand dollars. Is there anything you can tell me about the bank account that it was sent to from my joint account?" Ken crosses his fingers.

"Only thing I can tell you is it was sent to a foreign account, and I believe the country code is from Haiti."

After talking to the banker for a little while longer, Ken hung up and called J-Bo.

"Wassup, big bra?" J-Bo answered.

"Get a few guys out to Haiti. I think Nae and Tez may be there. This bitch been stealing money from me and sending it to an account in Haiti," Ken explained.

J-Bo frowned. "You thank dey really went there, big bra? Could just be a throw off," said J-Bo.

"Tez purchased a house there a few years ago. He has a girl and a daughter out there. I'll send you the address. I have to go through my old emails. I should have it in there because I helped him with the legal stuff when he bought it."

"Say less, big bra. Get me dat address and I'm on it."

"How's Flip?" Ken asked.

"He's aight. Just restin' up still," J-Bo answered.

***

Peanut danced with the choir the best he could on his wooden crutches. The Powder Springs congregation seated two thousand people and it was a full house. Tiffany sat on the front row in her best Sunday dress cheering and laughing at her man. Once the band had finished banging and beating and the choir stopped singing, the young, black pastor got on the mic.

"Praise the Lord," he said, taking a few deep breaths and sipping from a bottle of cold water. He used a small wash cloth to wipe the dripping sweat from across his forehead.

"Y'all say I'm the youngest pastor, huh?" He wiped the rag hard through his short afro, seemingly trying to touch his scalp. "How many of y'all are familiar with brotha Peanut?"

Almost the whole congregation cheered. "Brotha Peanut has been with us here at Trinity Chapel since he went through his tragedy. This brotha was put in a position where he had weapons placed to his head!" he shouted, putting his hand to his head like a gun. "And the men behind the weapons were ruthless and didn't care too much about taking his life." The pastor walked back and forth, looking in everybody's eyes. "Brotha Peanut wanted out of a gang. He knew that could've been the night he died. But his love for the Lord is so strong; so intense, that he took that chance." He wiped his forehead again. "How many of you today, if a group of terrorists ran into this church right now armed with automatic weapons and walked up on you…" He stepped off the four-step stage, randomly approaching a man seated on the first row, and placed his hand on his head.

"Put a gun to your head and said, you living for Jesus or not?" He stared at the man. "And whoever say yes…. the gunman pulls the trigger and moves on to the next person. How many of you would say yes?" He got quiet for a minute, went to give Peanut a hug. They both cried. "Peanut, I love you, brotha," the pastor said, handing Peanut the mic. Peanut talked and talked, giving his testimony about everything he went through with Young Boss.

Looks familiar, he thought, making eye contact for the third time with a woman seated in the middle row. After his testimony, everybody hugged, kissed, and said their goodbyes.

"Hey!" The pastor got back on the mic. "We've been calling him Peanut for so long don't nobody know his real name." Everybody erupted in laughter as they exited.

"You hungry, babe?" Tiffany asked, helping him into their SUV that Ken said they could keep.

"Yea," he answered, getting comfortable and clicking his seatbelt. Tiffany laid his crutches on the backseat then got behind the wheel and entered the road.

"I feel like it was somebody there I knew," he said, taking off the hat that covered the bandaging.

"We know everybody there," Tiffany said, looking from the road to him. She gently rubbed his head then his chest.

"No. Somebody I haven't seen in a long time."

"Baby, we're passed all that. We not about to stress ourselves out about it okay, love?" she said, turning into Popeye's Chicken. They ordered, then took it home to their two-bedroom house not too far from the church.

"Dang, big boy, you was hungry, huh?" Tiffany laughed from across the table. Peanut demolished the fried leg quarters. She was still biting at her piece. The bucket of ten pieces sat in the center of the table.

Peanut was reaching for another one when he bust out laughing. "I'm starving girl."

"So, how much longer before they say you can start Bible class?" she asked, sipping her sweet tea.

"They said the new class doesn't start till the first." He struggled to speak with a mouth full of chicken.

Thud!

They heard a light thumping sound from somewhere in the back of the small house.

"You heard that?" she asked.

"Yea. Go see what's up," he said. Tiffany went to the back. Peanut limped over to the small three seat sofa that sat in their plain living room and lifted the cushion. There was a 870 Remington pump.

"Aht aht aht," he heard from behind him. Quickly spinning around there was Tiffany and another lady about a foot behind her. She was dressed in all black. Peanut instantly recognized those big dark glasses the lady wore. She removed the glasses and those were a pair of eyes he couldn't forget. The slim, light skinned woman, wore a dark brown trench coat and a gun with a silencer hung towards the ground.

"I didn't come here for violence, Peanut. But if you pick up that shotgun, I'm gonna be forced to shoot you," Nae said from behind Tiffany.

Peanut shook his head and dropped the cushion over the gun and sat on top of it.

"Sit next to him," she told Tiffany. Tiffany obeyed.

"Listen Nae. J-Bo and Ken told me I was good. I shouldn't have no issues with nobody," he said, reflecting back on that night he thought he and Tiffany was about to die.

"Peanut, I don't care about any of that." Her voice was too soft for a violent burglar. She sounded desperate. She looked around their living room. It wasn't much of nothing; a couch and a TV.

"So why are you here breaking into my home?" Peanut asked.

"I broke in because if I would've knocked, I'm sure Ken would know I'm here by now," she said squatting down, dropping her head. She laid her gun down on the ground.

"Peanut." Nae looked up at him. "I need to ask you something and I need you to be very honest with me." She didn't break eye contact. Peanut looked at Tiffany.

"Look Nae, he's been through a lot; head trauma and stuff. How about you ask me instead," Tiffany chimed in.

"You wouldn't know. Peanut was there. So he'll know."

"Know what, Nae?" Peanut asked.

Nae took a deep breath. "I want to know exactly who shot me, and who killed my little sister." Her voice cracked when she mentioned her sister.

Peanut thought back to that night ten years ago. He stared harder at Nae's face and he could still see the scar on her chin from the bullet.

"Nae, what are you talkin' about?" He played dumb.

"Peanut, I already know Ken is the one that had my dad killed. I found a fucking letter from my dad that Ken's bitch ass had been hiding from me. My dad sent it saying his roommate was Ken's best friend, which is J-Bo. Ken didn't want me to know because for a long ass fucking time I had no idea he was into that type of shit. I've been thinking he's Mr. Goodie Two shoes and this nigga is really a whole fucking murderer, drug dealer, and gang leader!" she cried.

Peanut silently looked at her.

"Talk to me, Peanut," she said.

"Nae, I swear. I don't remember," he pleaded.

"Swear to God?"

Silence.

"Nae, I'm not going to put anything on God," he replied. His hands began shaking.

Nae snatched the pistol from the ground and jumped up in the same motion. She aggressively approached the couch and pointed the silencer at Tiffany's torso.

"Peanut, I swear to God. I swear on my dead sister's grave. If you don't give me a fucking answer, I'm about to empty all these shots in Tiffany in front of you!" Her crying was nonstop now. "Who shot me?"

"Me," he hesitated.

"Who killed Diamond?"

Silence.

"Peanut, who the fuck killed my little sister!" She raised the gun to Tiffany's face.

"Tez," he mumbled.

CHAPTER 12

"Haiti?" Asia said after he hung up his call.

J-Bo nodded. "Big bra, say, dat nigga Tez been had a house in Haiti." He was typing something into his phone. "Say he want a few people out there to watch out fa Tez."

"Any of us going?" she asked.

J-Bo shook his head. "Hell nah. We focused on a mission. I'ma send a couple of the youngins."

"But if they're in Haiti, that mean we would have to go there to complete our mission, right?" Asia asked, trying to make sense of it.

J-Bo grinned. "Dat nigga not in no fuckin Haiti, shawty. I just don't believe it."

"Me neither," Ty-Ty added, making a right turn at a red light.

"But that would only make sense. Get the fuck out of dodge, right?" she asked.

"Yea. But Tez gone fuck around and slip up. He's one of dem niggas dat think he's smarter dan everybody. Think he got all da fuckin sense. Dat boy ain't left da country. Prolly ain't left da city." J-Bo looked at Asia. "Aye, bra, you got a trail on Snag?" J-Bo asked Ty-Ty.

Ty-Ty nodded. "Yea. He'll call me if anything looks funny," Ty-Ty ensured.

***

Shakeena was at the local Big Lot's buying miscellaneous shit for the house; cloths, eating utensils, toilet tissue, etc, when her phone rung. She talked for a minute then hurried to checkout. She then went home to drop the items off before calling J-Bo.

"Ya?" he answered.

"You alright?" she asked.

"Yea, was just thanking bout JJ. You called yo mama or we gotta take a trip and go get em?"

"No, baby. She's going to bring him. But Kimberly just called me."

"What she say?" He asked so fast his words sounded blended together.

Shakeena laughed. "She asked could I meet her at the shop. She said all the equipment is about to be moved to Miami, and she wants me to help her drive the stuff there. That's going to be the new location."

"I knew dem mothafuckas wasn't in no gotdamn Haiti!" he exclaimed. "Okay, go do it. I'ma be following you."

"Okay," she answered before hanging up.

"Who was that boss?" Ty-Ty asked from behind the wheel.

"Keena. I knew damn well Tez ain't dumb enough to go back to Haiti, knowin' damn well Ken know where da spot at. But…" he shrugged his shoulders. "Dat's what Ken want. So I'ma send somebody out there," he laughed.

"So, what we doing?" Ty-Ty asked.

"Let's go by da salon. I wanna stay close. We followin' dem all da way to Miami even if we gotta get a hotel room and just go by the spot every day until Nae or Tez pop up." He decided the plan.

***

Thirty minutes later, Shakeena arrived at the plaza in one of the black Young Boss issued SUV's that J-Bo had given her. She parked in front of the salon. There was a big U-Haul truck in front and a few local movers were moving all the heavy hair equipment onto the truck. There were a few men on the roof taking the sign down. Shakeena got out and scanned the half full parking lot for Kimberly.

There were many people walking in and out of the dollar store, going to and from their vehicles. Some seemed to be just standing around watching the movers.

Where this girl at, Shakeena thought, walking towards the big truck. She wasn't there. Shakeena went inside the salon after two men came out carrying a big, thick, mirror.

"Kim!" she called, stepping inside. There were several workers inside taking stuff loose.

Damn! That nigga taking the sink off? Shakeena thought. She walked through the crowd of people and headed towards the back. Kimberly was in the back on the phone. Shakeena waited until Kimberly hung up before entering the room.

"What's up, boo?"

"Heyyy girl!" Kimberly exclaimed, giving Shakeena a big hug. "I'm glad you made it."

"Yea. My boo thang let me borrow his truck for a couple days."

"Okay, bitch, I see you. And who is he?"

"Bitch, bye!" Shakeena laughed. "I been fucking on this nigga for over ten years. His ass just been in jail, that's all."

"Okay, bitch. That's what's up. That jail dick good?" Kimberly asked.

"Girl, shut da hell up," Shakeena said before they both laughed. They walked through the salon, stopping where the men were working.

"They gone be finished in like two or three hours. I already paid everybody. I'll pay you once we make it to where we need to be. Is that cool with you?" Kimberly asked.

Shakeena fanned her off. "Yea, girl. You know I'm not tripping on that."

"You can drive this?" Kimberly pointed to the U-Haul truck, as they stepped out the salon.

"Yea, what you gone drive?" Shakeena asked.

"I got my van jam packed with all the smaller shit. But if you more comfortable driving my van, you can. And I'll drive the U-Haul," she said, looking into her phone.

"It don't matter to me, Kim." Shakeena smiled.

Kimberly gave her the key to the U-Haul.

"Oh, shit, bitch. I got a dick appointment I can't miss." Shakeena frowned. "What? right now?"

"Yes! My nigga works a lot. So when he say he's free, I gotta jump. Can you please stay here and watch them? It won't take long. Maybe like an hour and a half, and I'll be back."

"Okay, I got you. But what if they finish before you get back?"

"They won't." Kimberly climbed into the van and drove away.

"Where da fuck her big ass going?" Ty-Ty thought aloud.

"Huh?" J-Bo asked from the backseat. He was stretched out in the back, dozing off.

"Big girl just got in the whip and swerved," Ty-Ty said.

J-Bo sat up and called Shakeena. "Where da hell she go?"

Shakeena laughed. "This crazy girl talking about she got a dick appointment. She said give her about an hour and a half and she'll be back."

"She didn't say who da nigga is?"

"No," she answered.

"Aiight," he said before hanging up.

"Where she went?" Asia asked from the passenger seat.

"Talkin' bout a gotdamn dick appointment," J-Bo said, laying back in the seat.

"Shouldn't we follow her?" Asia asked.

J-Bo closed his eyes lids. "No. She'll be back. I'm sure."

Ty-Ty's phone rung. "Hello?" he answered. He listened for a minute. "Alright, just watch him. Thank you, bro." He hung up.

"Who was dat?" J-Bo asked.

"Lil bro. He said Snag been parked outside of a house in North Atlanta for about thirty minutes," Ty-Ty answered.

"Ty-Ty! That's where we followed this bitch to that night when I kept saying Snag is lying and I thought he was in that girl house! It was North Atlanta!" Asia exclaimed.

J-Bo sat up. "Are you sure?" he asked.

"Yes!" Asia remarked.

"You remember exactly where y'all was at?"

"Yes!" she said.

"Let's get it, Ty!" J-Bo said, sitting straight up.

***

Half an hour later, they pulled up to the neighborhood, parking next to the other Young Boss truck in the two car driveway. The medium sized house was for sale. They were a few houses down from Kimberly's. Asia rolled her window down and the driver of the other truck rolled his down also.

"Young Boss, Young Boss, 25-2, I'll neva cross," Asia said to the young boy behind the wheel. He was skinny, light-skinned, and kind of favored the rapper, Webbie, with that little afro he sported. He had to be about eighteen. He repeated the greeting.

J-Bo smiled, looking at Asia.

"Snag in there?" she asked.

"Yea, he in there sis," his voice was mature.

"By himself?" she asked.

"Nah, some girl just pulled up. I guess it's her house because she unlocked the door."

"The girl skinny or fat?" Asia had to be sure.

"She a big girl," he said.

Asia looked back at J-Bo.

"You a grown boss. I'ma let you call all the shots right now!" He smiled, loving the fact that she took initiative.

"Okay," she said turning her head back to the young boy. "You stay right here. Just be our eyes and ears."

The young boy nodded. Asia hit the button on the volume knob and pulled a pistol. J-Bo did the same. Ty-Ty already had his on him.

"It's a possibility that Nae and Tez could be hiding in here planning on going to Miami inside that U-Haul. So be on point," Asia said.

"What's da plan, boss?" J-Bo asked, biting his tongue, trying not to smile.

She pulled the rubber band from her wrist and tied her long hair into a ponytail. "You and Ty-Ty kick the front door. It's a thick wooden one, but with the right amount of pressure under the doorknob, it'll open with no problem. We're most definitely coming out of here with Snag." She looked at J-Bo, then Ty-Ty. "I guess y'all believe me now, about him being in this house that night?"

Silence.

Ty-Ty pulled right next to the stuffed minivan Kimberly was driving. They all exited the truck, guns drawn. Ty-Ty put the gear in park, leaving the engine running. Asia quickly approached the van, looking through the windows; nothing but hair supplies. She motioned towards the house. They all approached the front door. Asia looked back a few times for neighbors of any sort, but there was nobody. Asia gave a slight head nod and Ty-Ty and J-Bo's feet both crashed into the door about an inch under the deadbolt. The door swung open.

Asia squeezed through them and was in the house first. Her gun was trained, just the way J-Bo had taught her. The living room was dark, and smelled like ass. There was a big sectional couch they had to walk around before getting to the bedroom. Directly to the left of the couch was a small kitchen, and a bathroom next to that. The door was already open. Nobody was in there.

"Fuck me, daddy!" Asia heard moaning coming from the room with the closed door. They all squatted down. Asia approached the door. As she got closer the moaning had ceased. There was movement in the room that was a little too fast and aggressive for a tired person that just finished fucking. She moved backwards into the guys, fanning them to take cover behind the couch. "They know we here!" she exclaimed as quiet as she could.

"What?" J-Bo whispered back, as Asia pushed him into Ty-Ty. Both of the men took cover behind the couch. Just as Asia was covering under the barstool in the kitchen, the bedroom door snatched open. Asia held her index finger up to the guys. They waited patiently for a few seconds. Asia peeped her head around the corner to see Kimberly standing in the doorway naked, scanning the living room. Her wide breast hung down to the middle of her stomach, and her stomach covered her pussy.

"Somebody out there!" Kimberly screamed, running back into the room. Just as Asia stood up, a gun went off from the room. J-Bo stuck his arm around the corner and let off three shots blindly. Asia ducked just in time. That first bullet was inches from her temple. Asia gave a strong nod to the left, instructing the men to handle that. She took off, going through the patio to see if anybody was trying to escape through a window. Nobody was. Returning to her position under the barstool, the gunfire was still going. Asia propped her gun on the floor and aimed it low as she could, then squeezed the trigger.

"Ah, fuck!" someone squealed from around the corner, and the gun fire stopped. Asia instantly jumped up and turned the corner. Snag was on the floor holding his ankle, blood seeping through his fingers. His gun was inches away from his hand.

"I thought you wasn't in this house," Asia asked aggressively, kicking the gun away from him. J-Bo and Ty-Ty was right behind her. Snag dropped his head, not able to hold eye contact with J-Bo.

"Get him in the truck," Asia ordered.

Ty-Ty threw Snag over his shoulder and carried him out.

Asia entered the room with J-Bo on her heels. Kimberly was struggling to put her pants back on.

"Where the fuck is Nae?" she asked.

"I don't know! I swear!" Kimberly cried.

Asia stepped closer to her. "How the fuck you don't know and you handling all of her business? Bitch you better give me a phone number or something!"

"I swear I don't know! That girl send me postcards from different places and tell me what to do every time," she explained.

"Where da postcards at?" J-Bo chimed in.

"I throw them away every time," she said, closing her eyes when J-Bo trained his gun on her.

"What's up, boss?" he asked, looking in Asia's eyes.

***

They pulled into the warehouse that looks like a recording studio on the outside. There was a small Honda parked by the front door already. Ty-Ty floored the gas pedal until he was beside the small car. He threw the truck in park and pulled Snag from the back, tossing him over his shoulder again. Asia and J-Bo were behind him.

"Who's this?" Asia was pulling her pistol as the small car's driver's door opened. J-Bo grabbed her wrist.

"Chill out. Dats da doctor," he said, taking the keys from Ty-Ty and running to unlock the warehouse.

Once inside, Ty-Ty laid Snag down on the ground and the doctor attended to his ankle.

"Ahhh!" Snag screamed, clutching his fists. The doctor was using an instrument to pull out the rest of the chipped off bullet that was still in his ankle. He finished quickly and poured a lot of peroxide in the wound. The doctor wrapped Snag's ankle. He was done in about ten minutes.

"How much I owe you?" J-Bo asked.

"Uhh, about five grand," the doctor replied, cleaning his hands with some foam substance he had in a plastic bottle.

J-Bo ran upstairs, disappearing on the top tier, and was back in a few seconds. He gave the doctor the money. The doctor packed his briefcase looking tote and left.

"You working wit Tez and Nae, shawty?" J-Bo asked calmly, standing over Snag.

"Man, fuck no, J-Bo! Come on big, bro! You know me betta than that!" Snag snapped.

"So what the fuck were you doing in that bitch house after you swore up and down you didn't know the bitch?" Asia questioned.

Snag grimaced her. "Man, listen!" Snag wiped his face. "I been fucking that bitch for years; way before she even started doin' hair and got cool wit Nae. I tried to hide it because I know for a fact it would make me look suspicious. And I know for a fact shawty don't got no contact with Nae. She won't lie to me. Nae be sending her postcards from different cities and shit with no return address. I been playin' it cool, tryna catch the bitch slipping one day."

"So that night you made me look like a fool, you really was in her house?" Asia asked.

Silence.

"Respect rank, nigga!" Ty-Ty barked, crashing his size fifteen shoe into Snag's ankle.

"Ahhhhhhh!" Snag cried, expressing excruciating pain. "Yes. I was in there that night."

CHAPTER 13

A few days later…

"I apologize, sis," Snag said, while holding the lever at the top of the truck's door to help him slide in. Asia was carefully guiding his right leg into the vehicle. She threw his crutches in the back and got behind the wheel.

"Apologize for what?" she asked, strapping her seat belt. She hit the button on the volume knob.

"For lying to you." He reached under the seat when the spot opened and laid the 9mm on his lap.

Asia sighed, starting the ignition. She looked at him, merging into traffic. " I still don't get it. You could've said all that from the beginning." She shook her head.

"I know, but…" he dropped his head. "I know how these niggas rock."

"How who rock?" she asked.

"Young Boss niggas," he answered.

She looked at him when traffic slowed up. "What the hell does that supposed to mean?"

"These niggas wouldn't buy that story. They woulda thought I was lying, sis."

"Okay. Imagine how that shit makes you look now. That shit made you look suspect as fuck, bra," she said.

He let his head hang. "Yea, I can imagine." He looked at the gun for a while then back up. "You really believe I would lie about that and be holding back information on Nae and Tez?" he asked. He then picked up his phone, typing something.

"Snag, I don't know what's going on, bra."

"I been Young Boss long as I could remember. And for y'all to think some shit like that… that shit hurt, sis." His voice was softer than earlier.

"Ain't nobody said nothing about that. You're the one saying shit." She made a turn. "Didn't you say you knew about a backstreet or something to get us to the bluff quicker?"

"Yea." He was on his phone while riding through the bluff, trying to figure out a new spot to set up shop in, per J-Bo.

"What da fuck?" Snag thought out loud as they were leaving. He was staring at a car they'd passed already like a guard dog does an intruder

"What?" Asia asked, snapping her neck to him.

"Hold up, hold up!" He turned as much as his body would allow without hitting his ankle against the door. "Slow down, sis."

"What's up? What you see?" she worried.

Once Asia slowed down the small BMW rode pass them.

He flicked the safety off the 9mm and slapped one into the head.

"Get on da otha side of them!" he wolfed.

Asia stepped on the peddle, picking up acceleration. She swerved to the left, and sped up until she was side by side with the small luxury car.

"I knew I'd catch these mothafuckas!" Snag exclaimed, holding the switch on his door to automatically roll his window down.

"Wait Snag!" Asia shouted.

He looked at her crazy. "Wait?"

"Who the fuck is that?"

"Tez and Nae!" he hollered back before stretching his arm out the window. The driver of the BMW had to have seen him because the instant his arm came out the window, the small car begin to speed up.

"Speed up!" Snag called to Asia.

Pop! Pop! Pop! Pop! Pop! Pop! Pop! Pop!

He sent eight shots through the driver side window. The car started to swerve wildly. The driver was clearly injured.

The car straightened, and Asia drove as fast as she could on the slim road. Looking through the window, the driver wasn't moving. His foot was clearly still on the pedal. The female passenger was steering, and struggling to move his foot. Once equally side by side with the small car again, Snag let the rest of the clip fly into the car, planting them into the dead driver and the passenger.

Asia slowed a little and the BMW went turning rambunctiously, hitting the sidewalk at an angle. The small car flipped, spinning multiple times, before landing straight up.

"Hold up!" said Snag, feeling Asia about to drive off. He reached between her legs under her seat, grabbed the pistol, and struggled out the truck. He limped to the car about ten feet away, stuck his arm in and emptied the clip. He limped faster back to the truck. He was grunting and making funny facial expressions, clearly in pain.

"Gotdamn, Snag" she snapped.

"What?" He was cleaning his prints off the gun with the bottom of his shirt.

Asia stepped on the pedal. "Take that shirt off. You got blood all on the sleeve," she said.

***

The next morning...

"Can you please just leave all that stuff alone and stay here with me?" Zaya asked, sitting on the end of the bed massaging Ken's shoulders. He sat between her legs.

"That's the plan. I just have to ensure something happens before I do," Ken said. His eyes were closed. He rested his head back, enjoying the relaxation.

Zaya leaned her head over and gave him an upside-down kiss on the lips. The kiss was a few seconds longer than the peck on the lips he got before. She took a few seconds to suck on his lips. He opened his eyes. She smiled.

"What?" she asked, already knowing.

"You never kissed me like that before." He was shocked.

She looked up, smiling. "Maybe I'm starting to like you more."

"Maybe you're starting to like me more?" Ken laughed. "Just maybe? But you want me to live with you, and you maybe, like me more? Make it make sense, baby." He unhooked the thick white robe from his shoulders, allowing it to drop to the ground. Zaya was able to massage more down his chest.

Still smiling, she said, "I know what I want, Kenneth." Her hands traveled farther down his chest. She twirled her fingers around his nipples, pinching them. She squirted more of the essential oil in her hand before pinching his nipples again. She grabbed a towel and dried the back of his shoulders.

"Get on the bed, babe," she instructed.

Once on his back she mounted him. His Nike shorts and her thin panties pressed together so that they were feeling each other. She rubbed down the center of his chest, slowly maneuvering her slippery hands, covering the top of his stomach region.

"All of these damn tattoos," she said, tilting her head in different directions to see the tattoos clearly.

"I was young," he said, eyes still closed. "I've been thinking about removal."

She slowly grinded upwards. His body flinched. She did it again.

"Don't remove them," she said softly.

"Why not?" He opened his eyes.

"They're sexy," she said, grinding again. "Uhmm," she slightly moaned, feeling his dick go from gummy worm to brick really quick. The fabric of his shorts was thin. Her cotton panties were even thinner, so it almost felt like he was attempting to work himself inside of her.

Finally about to get some, he thought.

She scooted down his legs and pulled his shorts down. His dick stood straight up.

"What you giggling about?" he asked.

"Because I just realized you're a freak. Why don't you have any drawers on?"

He smiled. "It's hot."

She laughed. "It is not that hot." She gently hit his chest with a closed fist. She applied more oil to her hand.

"You like that?" he asked after she gripped his shaft.

"I love the thickness." She slowly applied the oil on him.

"And the length?" he asked, locking his fingers behind his head.

"Hmmm," she used her other hand to measure. "I'll say it's about seven, maybe eight inches. Length is fine. But I'm more of a girth fan. I'll rather have it short and fat rather than long and skinny." She squeezed his tip, maneuvering her wrist in all directions.

"Ahh," he moaned, staring in her eyes. "Oh, it get wet like that?" He felt the spot under his knee where she sat dampen.

She lifted up and looked at his leg. That spot was definitely wet. She smiled.

"Did I do that?" she asked innocently, stroking him.

"Zaya, baby, please. Get on top of me. I can't take this any longer."

"Aht aht aht. Don't rush me, Mr." She stroked him faster.

"I'm not trying to rush you, baby. It's just been two months since we've been dating, sleeping beside each other, planning things for the future, and still haven't had sex."

"I want you here with me," she said, taking one hand off his dick, and using it to massage his balls. "I don't want you in Atlanta forever. I want you to myself," she whined.

"Soon." He could barely get that word out.

"What do you have to handle before you can stay here with me? Something with your wife?"

He shook his head. His phone rung. He ignored it. It rung again. Zaya leaned up just enough to pull her panties off. His phone rung again.

"Hand me that," he said.

She got up and grabbed his phone from the dresser. "J-Bo?" she said, looking at it.

He held his hands out and she tossed it to him. By the time he got it, J-Bo had hung up.

"I'll call him back," he said, dropping the phone on the bed.

"Good idea," Zaya whispered, crawling on top of him. She grabbed his dick and massaged her clit with the tip.

"Uhhh, ummm, shit," she moaned.

You sexy as fuck, he thought,

"You going to fuck me, Ken?" She moaned, sliding his tip from her clit to the opening.

His phone rung again.

"Please give me two seconds," he said. "Hello?" His eyes bolted open. "I'm on the way!"

***

Two hours later…

"Last night there was a tragedy. Two victims; one male, one female, were gunned down on one of our streets here in Atlanta. They were overkilled. Thirty-two shots were let off at the two victims; twenty-four of which hit them. The guns caused so much damage to the faces of the victims, they were considered unidentified. Later the car was searched, and the patrol officers found identification. Nae Griffith and Martez

Challey were brutally murdered. At this time we have no suspects. Reporting live, Atlanta news," the news anchor said before J-Bo hit the button on the remote cutting it off.

They were all in the warehouse in Atlanta. They'd setup a projector and allowed the news recording to play on the wall. By the time Snag hit the light switch, Ken was in tears. J-Bo, Ken, and Asia stood on the top tier. Snag and Ty-Ty stood at the bottom. Ken sat up from his seat and hugged Snag.

"How did you track them down, Snag?" he asked after the embrace.

"Big bra, we was just ridin'. I thought I was trippin' or some shit. I told sis to speed up to make sure I wasn't trippin'." He shook his head. "This nigga, Tez, looking right at me. I came straight out the window and clapped em," Snag explained.

"Where exactly were y'all?" Ken asked.

"Leaving the bluff," Snag answered.

"She was scared?" Ken asked, nodding to Asia.

"Nah. She handled that shit like a real G." Asia smiled.

J-Bo looked up.

"I feel a little better now," Ken said.

"Just a lil? It's time to celebrate, big bra!" J-Bo exclaimed.

Ken shook his head. "I need to speak to y'all anyway." He took a seat in the chair that was always on the top range. "I'm tired. I'm ready to put all of my focus on this music business. I don't want to watch over my shoulder anymore. I'm moving to Texas and leaving Young Boss in the hands of J-Bo and Flip." Ken stood and hugged J-Bo. "J-Bo, I'm going to give you the contacts to another plug that I never exposed to you. So, you can keep everything going." Ken shook his head. "I'm so proud of y'all. J-Bo, I want $10,000 a month until the day I die."

"No problem," J-Bo said.

"I think he deserves a promotion." Ken nodded to Snag.

"He's definitely a grown boss as of now." J-Bo smiled to Snag.

Snag laughed hard.

"What happened to your foot?" Ken asked Snag.

"Long story, I'll fill you in," J-Bo said, walking off with Ken.

"J-Bo?" Asia called to him once they were all back in the parking lot outside the building.

He nodded his head, still escorting Ken into the truck.

That's weird as fuck, Asia thought.

After Ken was in the truck, J-Bo talked to a couple of the other guys that had picked Ken up from the airport. He instructed them on what to do and where to go. He was attempting to get in a different truck, when Asia called to him again.

"J-Bo!"

"What's up, man?" He threw his arms out, clearly irritated.

"What's the matter with you?" she asked.

"Nothing! Wassup shawty?" he asked quickly, looking down.

"You were just fine a few minutes ago. Why are you acting different?"

"Ain actin different. I just ain't tryna kick it." He looked at his watch.

"Okay, why you not treating everybody else like this?" She frowned.

He looked around the almost empty parking lot, mumbling something, then back to her.

"Shawty, you just had so much fuck shit to say about shawty," he said.

"About who?"

"Snag." He made himself clear. "You was just swearin' up and down dat shawty on some bullshit. And dis same nigga just handled dat business. Makes me wonda," he said, boarding his truck.

"Make you wonder what?" She was confused.

"Nun," he said before closing the door. The truck with Ken in it pulled off. J-Bo followed closely behind.

Snag came limping closer towards her. She ran to him, put her head under his arm and helped him to the truck.

"See how I lied for you?" Snag asked once they were both in the car.

"How the hell you lie for me?" Asia asked, staring at him.

"I told Ken you wasn't scared." he laughed. She didn't laugh with him.

"J-Bo was just treating me really weird," she said, starting the ignition.

"Don't think too much about it. He stressed out about Flip," Snag said.

"What's up with Flip?" she asked.

"He has to have another surgery. Something went wrong," Snag explained.

CHAPTER 14

"What you thinkin' bout Asia?" Smoke asked, entering the truck.

She shook her head. "J-Bo was just treating me really weird." Her head was cocked to the side.

Smoke leaned over and kissed her lips. He held the back of her head and kissed her genuinely, tasting each lip as well as her tongue before pulling back.

"You almost look like Smoke again," Asia commented, rubbing a finger down his face.

"The swellin' went down?" he asked, touching his face in different areas.

She nodded. "For the most part, yea." She kissed him again.

"So, how was J-Bo treating you weird?" he asked, sitting back in his seat.

"He just seemed like he didn't want to talk or hear what I had to say. Then he seemed like he was mad because I thought once upon a time that Snag was up to something slick." She threw her hands up. "Hell, we all thought that. J-Bo was the one that told me to keep an eye on him," she vented.

"I think I heard some extra shit happened with Flip. Some shit bout he need more surgery or something. I don't know. But just give him time. J-Bo's a aiight nigga." Smoke placed his hand on her thigh.

"You might be right." She let her seat back some.

"Where the hell is Snag?" He looked in the backseat.

Asia smiled. "Well, we weren't doing shit right now. So, he asked me to drop him off at a hotel because his baby's mama is coming into town. He don't want her to know where he really be at so he gone let her come to his room. He asked me to come back and get him in about two hours," she smiled.

Smoke laughed so hard he almost started choking. Asia had to pat him on the back.

"That nigga ain't got no mothafuckin baby mama. Got shit but some prostitutes," he said, laughing again.

***

Everything aiight, boss?" Ty-Ty asked from behind the wheel, not taking his eyes off the other truck he was following.

J-Bo scratched his head. "Sum ain't right wit' Asia. You think she was protectin' Nae and them?"

"Why you say that?" Ty-Ty asked.

"She was sayin' all dis slick shit dat Snag got goin' on. Now, look. He clapped both of dem mothafuckas."

"We all thought Snag was on some funny movin' shit, boss," he reminded J-Bo.

"Yea, I guess you right." J-Bo looked up. "Where da fuck dey goin'?" He looked at the truck Ken was in, and they were taking a turn they weren't supposed to. Ty-Ty sharply snatched the wheel to the left, trying not to miss the turn. He made it just in time. J-Bo called one of the men's phone inside the truck and snapped.

"Where da fuck y'all takin him!" he bellowed. The boy passed Ken the phone.

"It's cool, J-Bo. Peanut had been calling me. He just called again. I'm going to go see him before I leave town again," Ken said.

"Aight." J-Bo hung up.

"What's up boss?" Ty-Ty asked, ready to do damage.

"We goin' to see Peanut."

J-Bo frowned as they pulled up to the single story, Powder Springs home. He looked around. The grass was blended with dirt patches and there was a fence surrounding the front part of the house. The fence looked so weak, a child probably could break through it. A crackhead walked aimlessly past the house.

Dis shit look dirty as fuck, J-Bo thought.

"Ain't no way Ty," J-Bo said. "What da fuck kinda shit Peanut got goin' on?"

Ty-Ty shook his head. They both filled their hips with the 9mm's from under the seat before exiting the truck. J-Bo approached the truck where Ken was, knocking on the passenger window. The window slid down.

"Ken can't step foot out dis truck till we clear da place," J-Bo ordered. The men nodded. They easily pushed passed the fragile fence. Ty-Ty went behind the house. J-Bo knocked at the front door.

"J-Bo!" Peanut smiled, opening the door.

"What's up, bra?" J-Bo gave him a brotherly hug, looking into the house.

"Where's Ken?" he asked.

"We gotta do a security check. You know how dat go," J-Bo said. Peanut nodded, stepping aside, allowing J-Bo into the house. J-Bo instantly walked all the way to the back. Seeing Ty-Ty's shadow through the back door, he unlocked it. They searched the entire house, being sure to look under the bed and open all cabinets.

"Why y'all treating us like we're the ops?" Tiffany asked, when Ty-Ty made her stop cooking to put her hands on the wall for a pat down.

"You know how it goes, bae. Just chill out," Peanut said, standing beside her, getting patted down by J-Bo. Ty-Ty went and told the guys it was good. Two of them escorted Ken to the front door. Ty-Ty took over from there, entering the house with Ken, who looked around the living room. Ty-Ty took him into the kitchen where everybody was.

"Ken," Peanut smiled, hugging him.

Tiffany was at the stove. She turned around and hugged Ken next. He looked at the table then back up.

"Peanut, you needa tighten da fuck up, shawty. Dis small ass fuckin' table! You expect big bra to sit at dis shit!" J-Bo snapped.

Ken smiled. "It's aiight, J-Bo. I'll stand. What's goin' on with you, Peanut? Are you okay, bro?" Ken asked, looking around the small kitchen. He looked at the walls, the floor, and the stain on the outside of the refrigerator. Ken crossed his arms.

"I'm okay Ken," Peanut said, stepping a tad bit closer to Ken. He straightened out the collar of his loose t-shirt. "Ken, when y'all," he looked at J-Bo, then back to Ken. "Allowed me to walk out of that meeting that night. That was supposed to be it, right?"

"Yea, as long as you doin' just what you said: focusin on ya life with God. But if you get caught up gettin' active in da streets in any typa way, I'ma make sho you get spanked," J-Bo said.

"With all due respect, J-Bo," he dropped his head. "I need this question answered by the mega boss."

"He is the mega boss now, Peanut. I'm out," Ken said. Peanut's body slightly trembled. He looked J-Bo over. There was an arrogance about J-Bo that he wasn't feeling.

"My apologies, so…" he was saying.

"Peanut, what's up brother? I wanted to come and spend a little time with you. But your living conditions are…" he paused, conscious of Peanut's feelings. "You said you needed to speak to me. Here I am. What's up?" Ken was straightforward.

"Nae broke into my house the other day and pulled a gun on me and Tiffany."

"How would she know where you live," Ken asked.

"I don't know. She was at one of my church services." He looked at Tiffany. "Maybe she followed me."

"What she wanted?" J-Bo asked.

Peanut looked at J-Bo, then back at Ken. His eyes watered. "She wanted to know who shot her, and who killed Diamond."

"What you tell her?" Ken asked.

"I told her the truth." He said it like he was embarrassed.

"You and Tez?" Ken asked. Peanut nodded. Ken hugged him and Tiffany again and said his goodbyes.

"You ain't gotta worry bout shawty no mo," J-Bo said.

"Who?" Peanut asked.

"Nae. She dead," J-Bo said.

Tiffany gasped. "When did that happen?" she asked.

"Da otha day." J-Bo frowned.

"The other day?" Peanut asked in disbelief.

"Yea, why you say it like dat?" asked J-Bo.

Peanut shot Tiffany a look of uncertainty, and she shrugged. He looked back at J-Bo. "Nae called me today and told me she appreciates me for my honesty."

***

"See what I mean, sis? You gotta be on top of these niggas. These niggas will try to be slick and shit," Snag said, throwing the duffle bag in the back seat.

"Yea, I feel you. That's crazy how he just lied. Violation now, right?" she asked.

Snag flashed a half smile. "Nah, sometimes it's good not to violate niggas. It makes them feel like they owe you one. So, whenever you need them again, they won't hesitate."

"Makes sense." They rode around to a few of the spots, collecting money. One of the young niggas tried to cuff ten thousand. J-Bo told him to get all the money until it totaled two M's. He had to give Ty-Ty, Asia, J-Bo, Smoke, and Flip fifty thousand each because they were the ones putting in all the work to find Nae and Tez. Even though Flip's been in the hospital, J-Bo still made sure he got a cut.

"If it seems like too much pressure on that foot, just let me know and I'll drive," Asia said.

"Shit, I got it. This the only way to get it back right. I gotta get back used to doing simple shit like driving."

She nodded. "I'm hungry, bra," she said.

"Wanna go sit down and eat?" he asked, coming off of Camp Creek.

"Nah, stop there." She pointed at a Burger King.

"I don't like that one. Let's go to another one." He kept his eyes straight.

"No! I'm hungry, like my stomach is touching my fucking back. Stop there." She looked at him like he was crazy.

He sighed and turned. Asia ordered enough for her and Smoke.

"You don't want nothing?" Asia asked. Snag shook his head, still looking straight.

This nigga acting weird again, Asia thought.

"No! That'll be all thank you!" Asia called to the lady through the speaker.

They paid at the first window. Snag's hands had began shaking. He dropped the money in the process of handing it through the window. Asia watched him without saying anything. He drove up to the second window. He slightly leaned his seat back some.

"Thank you for choosing Burger King," the employee said, handing the food through the window.

This bitch is ghetto as fuck, Asia thought. She looked at the green and blue streaks this super black skinny girl wore in her hair.

"I'll be right back with tha drinks." Her voice was a bit too loud for the job. When Snag reached out to grab the bag, the girl leaned in a little. A frown covered her face as she walked away for the drinks. Asia looked at Snag. He continued looking forward.

"What's up wit dat mothafuckin money?" the girl asked, coming back to the window with two drinks, aggressively rolling her neck.

"What?" Asia asked, looking at her name tag. *Lameka*, she thought.

"That bitch know who the fuck I'm talkin' to! Come on wit dat mothafuckin money Snag! Because dat was some foul ass shit yo ugly, black, snaggatooth ass did!"

"I don't know you, shawty." Snag finally looked up at her.

"You lyin', pussy ass, nigga!" she screamed, throwing one of the Sprites at Snag's chest. The pressure from the drink instantly knocked the top off the cup, wetting his face with all the contents. A little splashed in Asia's face.

"You dumb bitch!" Asia was saying before Snag pulled off. "Man, go back, bra. I'll beat that hoe ass."

"Fuck that crazy bitch," he mumbled. Asia took the napkins from the bag to wipe her face, giving Snag the rest.

"Who is she?"

He wiped his face and neck. "I don't know that hoe from a can of paint."

***

"I guarantee the bitch was a prostitute, and that nigga hadn't paid her or some shit like that," Smoke said. He sat on the end of the bed and chewed through the bacon cheese burgers Asia brought him back.

"I don't know, baby." She came from the bathroom drying her face with a towel. "It's something about the rage and anger in that damn girl's voice, and how weird Snag started acting. Shit makes me think it's more to it," she said. She unwrapped her sandwich and didn't take a single bite.

"You lost yo appetite?" he asked.

"Yes. I want to know what the hell was just going on."

Smoke shook his head. "Did you catch her name," he asked.

"Yea. Her name tag said, Lameka."

"So, what you do is, call there and ask to speak to her," he said, chopping down some fries.

Asia picked up her phone, googled the Burger King, and called. Nobody answered. She called again to no avail.

"Baby, I have to go by there." She stood up.

Smoke looked at her. "Are you serious?" He shook his head.

"Yes. This girl threw a whole fucking drink in this man's face, babe!"

"Asia, I already told you what that was about!" Smoke was getting frustrated.

"And what if it wasn't!?" Her eyes watered, face turned slightly red.

"Whatever." Smoke stood up, downing the rest of his drink. He slid into his black house shoes, and pulled his .45 from under the pillow.

"Let's go," he said.

***

"These folks might fuck around and be closed, bae," Smoke said. Asia turned into the establishment. You could see a single person moving around inside, but the lights were dim, and not a single customer occupied the inside.

"It's ten at night, baby. Their walk-in part is closed," she said, driving around the building. "The drive thru is twenty-four hours," she said right before being asked to place an order. Smoke looked out the window in all directions, clutching his weapon. She ordered a drink.

"Hey, is Lameka in?" she asked once she pulled around to the window.

The young lady just looked at Asia like she was crazy. "Umm, no, she's not."

"This the same shift from like an hour ago?" Asia asked.

"Yea, but Lameka got suspended," she said.

"For how long?" Asia seemed desperate.

"Honey, I don't know." Her attitude was obvious. "We don't give out people information," she said, walking away. She then started talking to a heavy-set lady, who was looking at Asia through the small window.

"Hey, I'm Jackie, shift supervisor. Can I help you?" the heavy-set lady asked.

"Can you give me Lameka's number please," Asia asked.

"No ma'am. I can't give out employees' contact information," she said.

"Pay her," Smoke mumbled from the passenger seat.

Asia went into her pocketbook and handed the lady three hundred dollars. "I just need her number, please."

The woman took the money and walked away. A few seconds later, she returned, handing Asia a bag. "It's in there," she said, closing the window back.

Asia handed Smoke the bag and drove away from the window. He started eating the fries the girl had put in there. He pulled the single napkin out and saw that's what Lameka's number was written on.

"Is it in there?" Asia asked.

"Yea," Smoke answered, still chewing.

CHAPTER 15

The next day, J-Bo and Ty-Ty went by Ken's house and took pictures of it. Ken had told J-Bo where the deed was inside the home and told him he could have it. Ken had no plans on returning to Georgia, unless it involved finding his son or it was some business involving his record label and artists. Certain documents Ken requested to be mailed to him once he established a Texas address. J-Bo had considered moving into the big abode, but changed his mind.

He took pictures of the house so he could place it in *home for rent* ads. He hired a small cleaning business to come by and tidy the house up. It was clean for the most part, but there were still minor spots that needed attention.

"Let's slide to Keena spot," J-Bo said, after the cleaners had left. He and Ty-Ty got in the truck and rode off.

Ty-Ty turned the music down. "You haven't thought about Peanut?" Ty-Ty asked.

"Hell naw. Thought about him fa what?" J-Bo asked, looking out the window. "Dat lil ass, fucked up ass house." He shook his head. "Shawty should be ashamed of his damn self!"

Ty-Ty almost laughed. "Yea, he should. But I'm talkin' bout what he said, fam."

"What he say?" J-Bo looked at Ty-Ty.

"About Nae texting him that morning," he said, glancing at J-Bo.

J-Bo frowned. "Oh yeaaaa!" He sat up, dragging his words. "Damn, shawty, I wasn't even thankin bout dat shit. He said Nae texted him, right?" He searched his memory.

"Yea, fam, but the time he said she texted him, Snag had already killed the bitch."

"So what typa games really goin' on?" J-Bo scratched his head.

"I don't know, but I think it's worth looking into," Ty-Ty suggested.

J-Bo's phone rung. He talked for a few minutes then hung up. "Aye bro, take me by Keena spot."

On the way to Shakeena's crib, J-Bo gave Peanut a call. He asked him for the number that Nae allegedly texted him from. J-Bo called the number a few times and got no answer.

"Look, I want to show you something," Shakeena said. She was standing on the porch when Ty-Ty whipped into the driveway. She grabbed J-Bo by the hand and pulled him into the house.

"Dat shit nice. When dey brung it?" he asked, looking around the fully furnished living room. It fit the living room perfectly; just like in his dream. He shook his head.

"Yesterday, and what's wrong? Why you shaking your head?" she asked, getting all in his face.

"Dis da same way shit was set-up in my dream." He sat down on the couch.

"What dream?" she asked, sitting beside him.

He sighed. "The night I was sweatin' so hard in my sleep, I had a dream. Nae and Tez was tryna kill us."

She frowned. "Kill us? What the hell?"

"Fuck dat. I'ma deal with it. Dey brung all da furniture?" he asked.

"Yea, come see." She grabbed him by the hand again, giving a full tour of the downstairs area.

"What's dat smell?" he asked, heading to the stairs.

"Vanilla incense. You like it?" she asked, walking in front of him.

"Hell yea! Shit smell good as fuck." He grabbed a handful of her booty on the way up the steps. She swatted his hand away, and flashed a sly smile. She gave a tour of upstairs.

"They brought something special for this room," she smiled, standing outside of JJ's door.

"We ain't buy no furniture fa dis room. His shit was still in here," he said, thinking if he was tripping or not.

Shakeena opened the door and JJ was sitting on the bed. He was watching something on Nickelodeon, eating a bowl of Cinnamon Toast Crunch. He laughed at something that happened on the TV, and J-Bo's eye's watered. His innocent laughter touched J-Bo. This was his second time seeing JJ since he'd been released and their relationship had been awkward, to say the lease. He still called J-Bo uncle from time to time and it was a constant reminder of Shakeena's betrayal. It wasn't JJ's fault but it still hurt.

All dese fuckin years I been gone. Dis my baby, J-Bo thought. Shakeena squeezed his hand, and kissed his cheek.

"JJ!" she called out.

"Huh?" the little boy said, still looking at the TV.

"Look at me, crazy boy." She laughed.

He turned around and looked at her; then J-Bo, then back to Shakeena. He stared in J-Bo's eyes. J-Bo's heart began thumping harder. It felt like it was coming through his chest.

"Uncle J-Bo!" JJ yelled in excitement. He ran to J-Bo, dropping the bowl in the process. Before he could make it to J-Bo, Shakeena stepped forward and forcefully pulled him by the shirt. "Listen to me, JJ, and listen to me good, baby, okay?" she said. He nodded.

"You remember that talk we had?" she asked, mean mugging.

He looked at J-Bo, then back to Shakeena. "Yea." His voice was soft.

"Okay, so don't call him your uncle anymore." Her voice was stern.

"What happened to…" he was saying.

"I don't know, baby, and I don't care. This is your daddy, okay?" She pointed to J-Bo. He nodded. She released his shirt.

"Daddy!" he screamed, jumping at J-Bo with his arms out. J-Bo caught him. He squeezed J-Bo's neck tight. J-Bo squeezed his body equally as tight. J-Bo could no longer hold the tears inside his eyelids. They freely rolled down his face. Shakeena went and cleaned the cereal up that JJ wasted. She felt herself getting emotional and wanted to distract her mind. She snatched the blanket and sheets off of the bed, taking it to the laundry room.

"I love you, Junior." J-Bo's voice cracking.

"I love you too, daddy," he said, still squeezing J-Bo's neck tight. J-Bo didn't loosen his grip until he felt JJ's grip loosening. He put the boy down.

"Daddy, why you was in jail?" he asked, looking in J-Bo's eyes, not blinking.

Protectin' y'all? Fighting? Fuck it, shawty, tell em da truth, J-Bo thought. He took JJ by the hand and walked him downstairs. He looked in the freezer.

Damn, I thought it was somethin' in here, J-Bo thought.

"You like ice cream?" he asked.

"Yes," JJ screamed, jumping up and down. "And I wanted some so bad, but my grandma wouldn't give me any."

J-Bo frowned. "Why?"

"Because she said it's bad for my teeth." He smiled, showing a missing tooth far in the back.

"Come on." J-Bo grabbed him by the hand again. "Keena!" J-Bo called from the bottom of the steps.

"Yea?" She came down.

"We finna go grab some ice cream," J-Bo said.

"JJ be eating way too many damn sweets. One of his permanent teeth done fell out, sooo," she crossed her arms.

"Please mama!" His face turned up.

"Chill out," J-Bo said to the boy. He looked back at Shakeena. "Don't do me like dat, shawty. You know how important dis is to me."

She smiled. "I guess."

"This is ya uncle, Ty-Ty," J-Bo said, walking outside.
Ty-Ty was standing beside the truck.

"What's up, lil man?" Ty-Ty smiled, giving the boy a
high five.

"What's up, uncle." He jumped into the high five, very
energetic.

"What's yo name?" Ty-Ty squatted down and asked.

"JJ or Junior."

"How old are you?" Ty-Ty said, still smiling at the
boy's energy.

"Ten," he said, running closer to the truck.

"Awww man! Uncle, this yo truck?" His smile was big.

"That's yo daddy's truck."

"Awwww man!" He opened the door and climbed in.

"Why you driving my daddy truck?" JJ asked from the
backseat.

Ty-Ty smiled. "It's my job," he answered, merging into
traffic.

"Yo job is to drive?" he asked, laughing at Ty-Ty. They
all laughed.

At the ice cream parlor they sat outside and ate pecan
pie ice cream.

"Dis yo favorite kind?" J-Bo asked, holding his hand up
to block the sun rays from dancing in his face, also blocking
his visual of his son.

"Yep," JJ said, fucking his portion up. "Daddy, why
uncle Ty-Ty keep looking around like that?" JJ wondered
why Ty-Ty was standing outside the truck, watching the
world.

"Ty-Ty is my brotha, and my personal security guard,"
J-Bo said, licking his spoon clean.

"So that mean if somebody try to hurt us, Ty-Ty going to fight them?" he asked, twirling the spoon of ice cream around in his mouth.

J-Bo took a deep breath. "If somebody try to hurt us, Ty-Ty gon' kill em."

JJ stopped twirling his spoon. His eye's grew larger. He looked at Ty-Ty, then back to his dad.

"Kill them with a gun?" he asked. His face showed worry.

J-Bo nodded.

"Daddy, you never said why you was in jail."

"I killed some people," he said, scooping the last of his ice cream.

"Why?" JJ swallowed a thick lump of the cold deliciousness.

"Dey stole some money from me and my family." J-Bo was frank.

No sense in lying to the boy, he thought.

***

"Hey, you alright?" Asia asked, when Snag picked up the phone. She was just turning into the Pittsburgh community.

"Yea, I'm good." He stretched out, making a loud relief from the stretch. "Where you at?"

"Just pulled up in Pittsburgh." She parked in front of the blue house on Smith Street. "You ain't never call me back to come get you. I'm just checking on you, making sure you're alright."

"Yea, I'm good, shawty. You by yoself?" he asked.

"No. Smoke right here," she lied.

"Aiight, let me wake all the way up and get my shit together, and I'll hit you back," he said.

She went inside and did a trap check. She ensured the way the young boys were running it wasn't drawing any extra attention to the spot. She had the youngins count the money and work right in front of her, making sure it all was accounted for.

I don't understand why they got these fuckin boards over the windows. This shit looks ghetto as fuck, she thought. She found a glass company on her phone's internet and called. She gave an estimate on the size of the window and requested a quote. She told one of the youngins to put that much money to the side and scheduled for the company to install two front windows. She took most of the money with her.

A few hours later, she was done trap checking and collecting money from all of the spots. She took the money to the safe house and stored it where it's supposed to go. She'd just started thinking about Smoke. She was preparing to stop at the first Red Lobsters she saw, until she passed a Burger King. That instantly took her mind off Smoke, and onto Lameka.

How the fuck could I forget, she thought, looking and feeling around the passenger seat for that bag. She had to pull over and search the car. It wasn't there.

Fuck, she thought.

She dialed for Smoke. "Baby, what's that number?"

"What number?" he asked.

"The number that was in that Burger King bag," she retorted.

"Hold on," he said searching for it. "Had done fucked around and threw it away," he said before reading the number off to her. "If she answer and you plannin' on linkin', come get me or let me know where you at, shawty. You don't need to be alone in that typa shit. Really you ain't pose to be alone now, but I know you good."

"It's okay, baby. You just took a Tylenol three this morning. Get as much rest as you can, daddy. I'm fine," she said.

"Okay. Oh yeah, J-Bo told me the other day to make sure you get a license to carry ya strap," he said.

"Yes, he told me. I forgot. Okay, I will. I love you."

"Love you too," he said before hanging up.

After they hung up she dialed the number and got no answer. It rung all the way through. She called again. Again. Again. Again. And again.

"Heh fuckin lo!" a ghetto, hood rat voice finally answered.

Asia smiled, remembering that voice. "Lameka?" she asked.

"Who da hell is dih?" she asked, yawning.

"Hey, my name is Asia. I need to meet and talk to you about something important."

"How you got my number? And talk to me about what?" She moved around, sounding more awake now.

"I was the girl in the car when you threw that soda at Snag."

"Bitch fuck Snag, pussy ass. You actin' like you tryna check me bout dat fuck nigga or sum? Yea, bitch I stay on Camp Creek. Come all the way to the end; apartments called Stone Creek. Make the first left when you turn in the complex, bitch! I'ma drag yo stupid ass!" Lameka snapped, before hanging up the phone. Asia called back a few times and got no answer.

Let me apply for this shit so J-Bo will stop damn crying, she thought. She went online to a concealed coalition website and took a six question survey to see if she qualified for a multi-state concealed carry license. After that, was a ten-question quiz. She was approved and entered her address for it to be mailed. She merged into traffic, thinking about Lameka, knowing exactly where the apartment complex was.

As she approached the dead end, she hit the button on the volume knob and pulled the pistol from under the seat, ensconcing it between her juicy thighs. She turned into the complex and rode the hill. Making the left turn she saw a few kids running in the street, chasing a ball. Another child was blowing bubbles, and there were about twelve adults huddled up in the far corner. They all stared at the all-black truck with tints that you couldn't see through. She parked in the middle parking spot in front of the building.

She looked through the crowd of people, squinting her eyes, seeking Lameka, but couldn't spot her. One of the younger guys from the crowd approached the truck. Asia rolled the window down.

"Wassup? What you need?" he asked, scanning the truck.

She was looking behind him at the apartment directly across from where she sat. A few people were walking out. She was trying to see if any of them was Lameka. She noticed a slight movement from where the no older than twenty year old boy stood. Looking through her rearview, she seen someone bent down, approaching. She raised the 9mm on the boy.

"Tell ya boy, back the fuck up," she whispered aggressively.

"Hold up, Tank! She strapped!" The boy looked over and yelled at his homeboy who was trying to sneak up on Asia.

The young boy that was approaching stopped in his tracks and ran from the truck. The boy that was talking to Asia ran off, too. The crowd of adults started slowly approaching her, some of which, clutched their hands in their pants.

Let me get out of here before I have to kill one of these niggas, Asia thought, switching the gear to reverse. A slim, lesbian stud from the crowd approached the truck with both of her hands up, showing Asia she didn't have a weapon.

"Wassup love?" She flashed a shiny gold smile. "Why you out here pulling ya tool on my lil niggas?" she asked, looking down at the gun in Asia's hand, then looked at Asia seductively.

"They was trying to be slick. But I'm looking for Lameka," Asia said arrogantly.

"Oh! You the one calling talking bout you wanna fight Meka?" she laughed.

"I'm not trying to fight her. I need to talk to her about something," Asia said.

"I can't let you talk to her with that gun in ya hands, love."

Asia heard her passenger side door handle being pulled on. She quickly took aim at that window. There was the first boy she talked to pulling on the door handle but it was locked. Just when she had her aim on him, the gold teeth lesbian pulled a .38 special from her baggy pants pocket, planting the barrel in Asia's pretty long hair.

"Drop it," the lesbian said calmly.

CHAPTER 16

Kill the lil nigga, then duck, and turn around and shoot this skinny ass, aids patient looking ass wanna be man ass dike, Asia thought. No! This isn't the shooting range. These targets actually shoot back, she thought, lowering her gun.

"Give it to me," she said pressing her steel more into the back of Asia's head. The girl snatched the car door open and all of the people that were outside approached the driver's side door. "I said give it to me!" she barked raising her gun to Asia's forehead. "I tell you one moe time. I'ma kill you right here," she growled.

"Pop dat hoe, Squeek," one of the men from the crowd said.

"You know you fucking with Young Boss, right?" Asia spat fiercely.

The stud looked back to the crowd, then back to Asia.

"Hold up, Squeek. You gone get us all killed," one of the men said, snatching the gun from the stud.

"Young Boss, don't got females. Give me my fuckin gun back!" She yelled.

"I'm the first one," Asia said, heart racing. Sweat beads had formed on her forehead.

"We fuck with Young Boss, and got a good relationship with them," the man that took the gun from the stud said, pulling his phone from his pocket. "You know J-Bo?" he asked.

"Yea, that's big bro," Asia said, growing a tad bit more comfortable.

***

"Daddy, where you live at? I want to go to yo house," JJ said, as they rode away from the Bruster's ice cream shop.

J-Bo looked back at him from the passenger seat. "Ion really got a house yet."

"So, you sleep outside?" JJ asked.

Ty-Ty laughed hard as he cruised down the street.

J-Bo's phone rung. He looked at it and put it back down.

"No, I don't sleep outside," J-Bo said, smiling. His phone rung again.

"Who's that?" Ty-Ty asked.

"Squeek nem, prolly tryna re-up," J-Bo said.

"Want me to answer?" Ty-Ty asked.

"Ion really wanna say too much," J-Bo said, nodding to his son.

"I'll code it," Ty-Ty said, reaching for the phone the next time it rung.

"Yo?" he answered. "This Ty-Ty, he's busy. What's up?" Ty-Ty*zzz zzz zzz zzz frowned. "Yea, she official." He hung up.

J-Bo gave him a weird look.

"I'll tell you later," Ty-Ty said.

"Daddy, I want you to come live at my mama house," JJ said.

"Might as well," Ty-Ty said.

***

He hung up the phone. "Ty-Ty said she's official."

"Who the fuck is Ty-Ty?" Squeek asked.

"That big, old ass nigga that's always with J-Bo; the one you scared of," he said. One of the young boys laughed. He stepped closer to Asia.

"My bad, sis. I'm Dre. This my lil sista, Squeek." He pointed to the stud. "Shit be shell round here so we gotta be on point. But what's yo issue?"

"I'm trying to figure something out and really need to talk to Lameka," Asia explained.

"You don't got no smoke with her?" He raised an eyebrow. Asia shook her head.

"Go get her," he said to Squeek, playfully pushing her when she turned to walk away.

"But out of respect for us, you got to put that burner up," he said. Asia respected it and stuck the gun between the seat.

Asia chuckled seeing Lameka come from the apartment. *This hoe is so ratchet*, she thought, looking at the colorful hair, burnt black crusty skin, and big ass clown lips. Lameka came and stood in front of Asia, her arms crossed.

"Sis, my name is Asia. I promise I'm not here for no issues. I never said nothing about fighting you. I was just trying to talk to you about something," Asia introduced.

"I'm listening." She rolled her eyes.

"Can y'all give us a minute please?" Asia asked Squeek and the dude that still stood there. They backed away a few feet.

"Don't get it wrong. Snag is not my nigga. I'm Young Boss, and I didn't like how he didn't tell me what that situation at your job was about. Whatever he owes you for, I'll pay you. But I need to know what does he owe you for?" Asia's heart rate picked up.

"My pussy ain't free," she replied.

Fuck! Smoke, was right. I don't know why the fuck I was thinking it could've been anything else. This skinny leg bitch is a prostitute, and Snag is a trick, she thought.

"How much he owe you, sis?" Asia asked, reaching for the glove compartment.

"A hundred thousand."

Asia turned back to her and frowned. She looked at the girl from head to toe.

"A hundred thousand for some pussy? Be for real, sis!"

"Nah, he did some real lame ass shit is why he owe me twenty thousand."

"What he do?" Asia didn't break eye contact.

Lameka's eyes watered. "Can I sit in here with you?"

"Yea, come on sis." Asia hit the lock switch. Lameka climbed into the back seat.

"This bitch ass nigga set my cousins up." Her voice cracked. "They not my real cousins. Just been close friends forever, so we call each other cousins." She dropped her head.

"How he set them up, sis?" Asia's voice was passionate.

"He told them he got a lil scam going on. He said it's a bank account with half a million dollas in it. He said the bank account is in two people name, a husband and wife. This nigga said he got the husband and wife held hostage somewhere and for my cousins to go get a legal name change to the people's name on the bank account. Then after a few days they could walk in the bank, withdraw all the money, and close the account, and he would give them a hundred thousand each. So, once they did it, they had to wait for new ID's to come in the mail. Once they got their ID's, he texted them telling them he was in the Bluff, handling some business, and soon as he finished they would all go to the bank togetha. He told them to meet him there, and at some point, they both ended up dead." She dropped her face into her hands and cried hard.

Asia's eyes damn near popped out of her head as she listened to the story. Her hands begin to shake and sweat at the same time. It fucked with her conscious, listening to the girl cry.

"Sis, I swear to God, I'll give you that money today. But I need to take you to J-Bo right now. I need you to tell him exactly what you just told me." Asia was talking fast.

"Okay," she sobbed, wiping at her face. "Let me go put my tennis shoes on." She got out the car and ran to the apartment.

Asia dialed for J-Bo. "Why the hell was Squeek callin', askin is you official?" he answered.

"J-Bo, that's a long story. I swear it's about to make sense. I need to see you now! Like right now! I'm like thirty minutes away. Where are you?" She was excited.

"Keena house," he answered. Asia hung up as Lameka came jogging towards the truck.

***

Snag sat in the Motel 6 counting money on the table. The room was dim because the thick curtains covered the big windows. There were two girls in the bed sleep. He looked at them and shook his head.

Lazy ass bitches, he thought.

He had to recount a few times. "Bitch gon' get twenty thousand and be happy with it. And if she ain't." He shrugged his shoulders. "Kill that hoe, too," he thought aloud.

He walked over to the two girls, and smacked both of them on the ass.

"Get up!"

Both the girls woke up stretching and yawning.

"How much this room cost?" he asked.

"Four-hundred for the week," one girl said, in between yawns.

"A thousand for our hair and nails," the other girl said.

"And another thousand for our pussies. Because yo nasty ass like to fuck too much," the first girl said. Snag smiled. He went to the table where he was counting up at. He only had twenty-two thousand on him. He put twenty-five hundred to the side.

Meka stupid ass gon have to take nineteen-five, he thought, pocketing the money. He picked up the twenty-five hundred and walked back to the bed.

"You hoes better get up and do something today," he joked, handing the first girl the money, and kissing them both on the lips before walking out the door.

Punk ass bitch talking about she'll put the police on a nigga if I don't pay her, Snag thought, shaking his head as he approached the dead end apartments. He turned up the hill. Instead of making the first left, he kept straight.

I'm finna go see what's up with Tisha lil fine ass. He thought about a new girl in the apartments. As he was passing his turn, he looked to his left and saw Lameka climbing into an all-black SUV.

What the fuck? That look like a Young Boss truck, he thought, quickly hitting a U-turn, then smashing on the brakes, not wanting to be noticed. Seconds later, the SUV started to move. Once the truck turned right, heading out of the apartments, he vividly saw the driver.

"Noooo!" He screamed, beating the steering wheel with his stiff fist. "What the fuck are you doing, Asia!" he continued screaming. His words turned into psychopathic howls and noises.

J-Bo will kill me. He will torture me until I die, he thought.

"Not me," he said, hitting the button on the volume knob. He grabbed the gun from under the seat and drove in the same direction as Asia.

***

"This shit finna be all over today. I promise you, girl. I'm going to make sure you get that money you're owed for the loss of your cousins. I don't give a fuck if they yo real cousins or not. And that nigga Snag is gonna die today. I promise you. J-Bo nem gone kill him," Asia said, grinding her teeth together. She whipped out of the apartment complex.

"I knew something wasn't right from the jump when he first asked dem ta do dat stupid shit," she wept, still wiping at her eyes. "He asked me at first, but I told him hell no. The fuck I look like changing my name," Lameka cried.

Asia glanced at her, then back to the road. "It's gone be alright, Meka." She felt bad.

What the fuck was he thinking? How the fuck you gone fake kill some mothafuckas? What the hell you gone do later on down the line when the real people pop up? It's still gone look like you set it up, dummy! Asia thought, anxiously, driving a little faster than the speed limit on the rural road.

"Is that yo people?" Lameka asked, timidly.

"Huh?" Asia looked at her. She looked in the sideview, and through her window.

"Is who my people?" Asia asked suspiciously.

Lameka pointed to the rearview. Asia looked up.

Why the fuck is this truck riding my ass like this? Same kind of truck I'm in, she thought, stepping on the pedal to see if she was tripping or not. She wasn't. The truck was still on her bumper. She switched lanes just for proof, and the other truck switched lanes too, on her like glue.

"Open the glove compartment! My phone. Get my phone!" Asia's voice was hysterical.

Lameka got her phone. After entering her unlock code, she went to her call log. J-Bo's name was at the top of the list. Right when she was about to press call, they got hit from the back. The force from the truck behind her caused her phone to go flying from her hand into the windshield, slightly cracking the glass. The phone fell on the floor.

"Get my phone and call that last number I talked to!" Asia screamed, glancing up to the rearview mirror. The truck wasn't letting up. Lameka went down looking for the phone. She found it.

"It must've broke on the windshield. The screen is all black," she said, still crying.

"Fuck!" Asia hit the steering wheel. She switched lanes, seeing the Burger King that Lameka was suspended from.

"Where the fuck is everybody at!" Asia said, looking around the street and the Burger King parking lot. It seemed like nobody was outside. Just when she was about to shift lanes the truck behind her made a hard right turn into the back of her, causing her face to hit the steering wheel and the truck to spin in a full circle. She looked up and the other truck was ten feet away head on with her. She squinted her eyes, staring, but couldn't see through the dark tint.

"You bleedin', girl!" Lameka said, as a few trickles of blood dropped from Asia's cheek. She threw the truck in reverse, quickly turning down a wooded side street.

"If we can make it to the end, we'll be good. It's a main road. I know a lot of people are out," Asia said, looking back, stepping on the gas. She was keeping the truck straight, driving backwards as fast as she could.

"Asia!" Lameka screamed.

Lameka grabbed the wheel and guided the truck as straight as she could.

Asia snapped her neck towards the front of the truck and saw the driver in front of her coming full speed towards them on the small road.

"My gun!" she said, snatching the 9mm from between the seat. Asia stretched her arm out the driver's window and took aim at the truck as it got closer and closer. She squeezed all sixteen shots and the truck was still coming. Her bullets knocked the truck's windshield out. The driver of the truck ducked down and hit her head on. She had no time to brace herself or warn Lameka that they were about to get hit. The force instantly crashed Asia's head into the steering wheel again, knocking her out. Lameka's hand was snatched from the wheel. Her head slammed into the window on her side, breaking the glass. The truck spun out of control, crashing and stopping into a tree in the wooded area.

CHAPTER 17

"You had fun with your daddy?" Shakeena asked JJ, entering his room. He and J-Bo were laid in his bed, watching cartoons.

"Yea, and I like my daddy truck." JJ sat up smiling. "I want one just like that."

"Your daddy will buy you one." Shakeena nodded to J-Bo.

J-Bo shot a quick stare at Shakeena.

"And what that look supposed to mean?" she asked flirtatiously.

"Yea, daddy. What that look supposed to mean?" JJ mocked his mother with a raised eyebrow.

J-Bo couldn't help but laugh. "It don't mean nothin', my nigga. I'll buy you one."

"Daddy, you gone move in the house with me and my mama?" he asked staring in J-Bo's eyes.

Shakeena walked away.

"Dat's what you really want?" J-Bo asked.

"Yes!" JJ said, playfully disguising his voice.

J-Bo made him lay back on him until JJ fell asleep. J-Bo called Asia. It went straight to voice mail. He slowly and quietly slid from under his son and covered him with the newer bedding. Shakeena had made the bed when they were gone. He walked into the hallway and called Asia again; no answer. He sent her a text telling her to call him immediately. He entered the master bedroom, standing in the doorway for a few seconds, looking at the furniture.

Dat fresh furniture be smellin' good as fuck, he thought. He heard the shower water running and didn't see Shakeena.

"I should hop in there and fuck da shit out dis bitch. Take out all my frustrations and pains she done gave me ova all these fuckin years," he thought aloud, taking his t-shirt and long sleeve shirt off. Placing the shirts on the dresser, he noticed three small keys: one bigger than the other. He went into the bathroom.

"Keena!"

"Yes, baby," she answered, opening the sliding door of the shower.

"What these go to?" He held the keys up.

"The two smallest ones goes to that damn U-Haul truck Kim left me with. And the bigger one goes to that salon. Why you being nosy?" she asked, pressing her perfectly rounded titties against the glass. J-Bo laughed and walked out. He stuck his head in to check on JJ. He was still sleep. J-Bo closed his door and went down the steps.

"You heard from Asia?" Ty-Ty, asked when J-Bo came walking towards him.

"Nah," he said, pulling his phone out and calling her again. "Her shit prolly went dead. She said she was on the way. Just make sho you let me know when she pull up." He held they three keys up.

"I got you, boss. What's that?" Ty-Ty asked.

"Da small ones go to dat U-Haul. Da bigger one go to dat salon. Send a few of the guys in there to search da spot. Tell em be careful. Look over any and everything. Tell me if dey find anything." He dropped the keys in Ty-Ty's hand.

"We lookin' for anything specific, boss?" Ty-Ty asked.

"Nah, I just got a funny feelin about sum. Ion wanna speak on it too soon. Just tell em, anything. No matter how small or big." He turned and went back into the house.

***

"Man, you sure he didn't say do this shit at night?" Kaylin asked his twin brother, Jiles, through the window of the-all black SUV. Jiles had called him a few minutes ago and told him he was going to pick up some keys from J-Bo, and that they had to go search a place. Kaylin had just pulled up to the house.

"Get yo fat ass in and quit crying!" Kaylin teased. Both of them were five foot six, weighing around two-eighty.

"Nigga, we twins! You just a lil lighter than me, but, nigga, you fat, too!" Jiles remarked, climbing into the truck. Jiles had whipped his thick fuzzy dreads to the back of his head. His brother Kaylin sported a low cut. They had smooth skin and their noses were both fat.

"Bitches like light skin niggas, not no charcoal black nigga like you," Kaylin joked.

***

"What's up, big bra?" Snag answered.

"You with Asia?" Ty-Ty asked.

"Hell nah. I talked to her earlier. She was in Pittsburgh with Smoke. We was posed to link, but I fucked around and fell back asleep. I'm just getting back up," Snag said.

"Okay, say less, bro." Ty-Ty hung up and dialed for Smoke.

"Wassup Ty?" Smoke answered.

"Let me speak to Asia real quick bro," he said, pacing back and forth in front of Shakeena's house, observing down both sides of the street.

"I been calling her. She going straight to voicemail," he said.

"So, after y'all left Pittsburgh, why was she alone after that?" Ty-Ty checked.

"Ain been to no damn Pittsburgh. What you talkin' bout Ty?" Smoke asked.

Ty-Ty frowned. "You and Asia wasn't together earlier today in Pittsburgh?"

"Hell nah! Who told you that?"

Ty-Ty raked his thick fingers through his beard. "Somebody told me they thought they seen y'all. Let me hit you back." He hung up, dialing a different number.

"We here now bro," Kaylin answered.

"Before I sent y'all on that mission, where y'all was at all day?" Ty-Ty stood still, turning the volume up on his phone.

"Shiiid, we been trappin'," Kaylin said. Him and his brother laughed.

Ty-Ty shook his head, frustrated. "Where the fuck were y'all?"

"In Pittsburgh, bra. You know we be at the spot," Kaylin answered, more serious this time.

"Asia came by there today?"

"Yea, earlier," he said.

CLANK!

"What the fuck was that noise?" Ty-Ty asked, suspicious of everything now.

Kaylin laughed. "Fat-ass Jiles knocked something off the counter."

Ty-Ty clenched his fist. "Was anybody with her?"

"With who, bra?" Kaylin asked, half talking to Ty-Ty, half arguing with his brother.

"I swear to God. I'm going to personally violate you," Ty-Ty said, calmly.

"Oh you talkin' bout, Asia. Nah, she was by herself." He got serious real quick.

"You sure wasn't nobody in the whip with her?" he asked.

"Yea, I walked her to the truck. Wasn't nobody in there," Kaylin ensured.

***

Am I dead? I'm breathing. I can't be dead. I might be dreaming. No! I know I'm not because I wouldn't be this conscious of everything going on. Why can't I move? Am I paralyzed?, What the fuck is that smell, Asia thought, tears forming through her closed eyes. What is this? she thought, trying her best to pull her face away from the cold sharp feeling object. Her head barely moved, but as she continued to try, she made progress.

"Ahh," she moaned softly, feeling a sharp pain throughout the entire front side of her body. When she gained the strength to lift her head, the sharp pain instantly went away, but the aftereffects were still there. She moved her right arm; then her left. Her left arm was numb. She slowly felt feeling trying to come back in her fingertips. After using the little strength from weak muscles she had to sit up, she tried to open her eyes.

"Umm, it burns," she whimpered. She could open her eyes a little, but then she shut them back because of a burn. Every time she shut her eyes back she felt the sting even more. She gently touched her face.

"What is this shit," she whispered, feeling all kinds of debris on her face. She touched the bottom area under her eye and gently rubbed her index across it. There was something small and stubborn. She tried to swipe it off and that caused her to flinch in pain. That's the moment she realized it was a small piece of glass in her eyelid. She built up the courage to pull it out.

"Ahh," she squealed, feeling that sharp pain throughout her entire body. She dropped the tiny piece of glass and wiped at her eyelid. Holding her hand in front of her face, she opened her eyes. It didn't burn. There was a little blood on her finger tips but not much. It was dark, but not too dark for her to know she was on a flight of hard wooden stairs. There was a door at the top of the steps. Once the feeling was all the way back in her left hand she repeated opening and closing her fist. There was a dim light at the bottom of the steps. She slowly slid down, one step at a time. As she got closer to the bottom, she noticed something.

Continuing to scoot herself down to the bottom, she got closer to the object.

The fuck is that noise? she thought, looking around. It sounded like movement and snorkeling.

"Oh my God! Meka," she whispered, realizing that object was the girl she had picked up earlier that day. Lameka was lying on her stomach. Her head was to the left. Asia pulled on Lameka's shoulders, trying to see if her neck would swing loose. It didn't. She scanned the dim area for what was making that pig like sound but didn't see anything.

"Thank you, God. I thought her neck was broke," she said. She overlooked Lameka's entire body. The leggings she wore were ripped, exposing her butt cheeks and vaginal area. Her panties were ripped from the back. Asia dropped some tears. Lameka's foot was twisted; a hint of a bone almost popping through her skin. Asia touched her wrist. She sighed deeply.

Thank God, she thought, feeling a pulse.

Asia tried to stand up and the soreness sent her right back down.

Feel like somebody beat my body with a fucking baseball bat, she thought. She began massaging the stiff soreness in her legs until it was able to bare. She clenched her teeth hard together as she struggled to stand. Her legs were hurting like a mothafucka, but she stood. Looking around the basement, there wasn't much; an old couch, a tall steel cabinet, a few wooden tables. She stared at the two tables, approaching them, rubbing her fingers across them.

These tables are so familiar, she thought. Why the fuck are these raggedy ass tables so familiar? Where did I see them at? Where the fuck am I? she wondered. Walking slowly towards the steel cabinet, she tried to turn the lever, but it was locked. She limped over to the couch. Her hands were out in front of her in case she had to grab something to avoid falling; just in case her legs decided to give out in her. She sat on the end of the couch, taking a deep breath. That feces odor entered her mouth when she took a deep breath, changing from a smell to a disgusting taste. She gagged and puked on the floor.

"What the fuck is that smell?" she asked herself, walking back towards where Lameka laid. She placed the crack of her arm over her nose as the smell grew stronger. There was a closed door.

Oh my God, it's a fucking pig in here, she thought, knowing exactly what a pig sounded like. She slowly turned the knob and barely cracked the door open. There were three black wild boars, all standing around four feet tall and weighing at least two-hundred-twenty pounds. One of the animals was chewing something that formed a lot of blood.

Please don't let that be a body part, Asia thought, looking at the other two.

The other two pigs were fighting over something. She couldn't really tell what it was because it had been chewed on so much. But whatever it was left the animal's tusks covered in blood. Blood also covered the floor. Right when she was closing the door back she heard a faint sound; like a piece of metal falling against the scratched up hardwood floor. She looked back in the room and right in front of the pig's mouth that was chewing what she hoped wasn't a body part, was a blood and pig saliva covered wedding ring in the floor.

Oh my God! They gone feed us to the pigs, she screamed in her mind.

Asia ran over to Lameka and gently slapped the side of her face. "Lameka, get up." Her hands had begun shaking as the pigs made more noise. Just listening to them chewing, especially with her knowing there chewing a dead human; her nerves were uncontrollable. "Lameka, I need you to get up," she said a little louder that time. Lameka didn't budge. She checked her wrist again. She still had a pulse.

"Fuck this shit. I have to save myself," she mumbled, climbing the steps. She reached the door at the top and crossed her fingers, silently praying that it wasn't locked. It wasn't. She turned the knob slow and as she was about to push the door, she heard an unfamiliar voice in the distance getting closer. She quickly crawled back down to the same spot she woke up in, and reluctantly positioned her face and body on the steps the same way she remembered.

"Well, you already knew I keep a few guns down there motherfucker. If you were worried about that then you should've cleared it out first. But to be honest, I ain't worried about it," a man said, opening the door.

"I'm looking at them right now, brother. I promise you. They're both dead. And if they ain't, I promise you them boars is still hungry. I ain't fed them in a week and just gave them a little snack before these two got here. So you have nothing to worry about," the man laughed, closing the door back. "Okay, you snaggatooth, motherfucker. I love you too, brother," he said.

Snaggatooth, mothafucka? she thought. Snag? Please don't tell me. Aww, shit! He probably seen Lameka in the truck with me and knew for a fact there was no way of getting out of this one, she thought, placing an open palm against her forehead. She held her hand there hoping the migraine would magically disappear. It didn't. Once the voice got further away, she went back down the steps. Forcefully, she grabbed Lameka by the left shoulder and pulled her hard, making her roll to her back.

"Ahh!" Lameka moaned.

Asia quickly put her hand over Lameka's mouth. Lameka weakly scratched at and hit Asia's hands.

"Shh!" Asia whispered in her ear.

Lameka was trying to say something. Asia moved her hand from Lameka's mouth once she lowered her tone.

"Stop it, Snag. Get off of me please," she cried softly. Asia instantly cried, knowing why her leggings and panties were ripped.

If I make it out of here, I promise, I'm going to kill that mothafucka myself. Asia made a silent declaration to herself.

***

"Wasn't really shit in there, bro. We found a bunch of quarters and mail," Kaylin said, stepping from his truck in front of Shakeena's house. As they pulled up, Ty-Ty was already walking towards the curb to meet them. He handed Ty-Ty the mail. He tried to hand him the rolls of quarters, but he didn't want it. Using the light from the truck's opened door, he scanned through the mail. All of it was from a Florida address; mostly *notices of services*, and address changes, but the new address of ownership wasn't there. There were three postcards; all from Florida, all sent at different times. The address was the same on all three. The most recent one had a short note: "Bring my notepad from the back office. Wednesday. My house. 1 am. Love u, bitch."

Today is Tuesday, but by one in the morning, it'll be Wednesday, Ty-Ty thought. He kept the post cards and told the twins to throw the rest of the shit away. He called J-Bo's phone, telling him of the findings. J-Bo came outside.

"Let me see," he said, looking at the cards. The sun had gone away already, so he went back inside to read the postcards in the light. Reading the cards once more he pulled out his phone, found Ken's number in his contacts and gave him a call.

"Hello?" Ken answered.

"I just sent you some pictures. Tell me if dat's Nae handwritin'," J-Bo said.

Ken looked at his phone then answered. "Yes, but, I thought…"

"Yea, me too. I'ma deal wit dat later. I'm finna jump on dis now," he said.

Ken took a deep breath before hanging up the phone without responding. J-Bo went back outside.

"We finna handle dis shit tonight," J-Bo said.

Ty-Ty nodded. "What about Snag? Want me to kill him?"

J-Bo shook his head. "Nah, because Ion really know one-hundred percent. Dis shit is weird as fuck right now," he answered.

"Just play everything like it's cool?" Ty-Ty asked.

"Exactly, but we finna need a few people. I'ma be right back," J-Bo said, before going back into the house.

CHAPTER 18

"Yes, daddy! I'm yo nasty bitch," Nae moaned. Tez was on top of her stroking hard and deep. Her wrists and ankles were bound by stainless steel handcuffs to the top and bottom of the bed, making it impossible for her to run away from him. The pink fur on the inside of the cuffs is what kept her wrists and ankles from getting bruised. He planted his face into her neck, sucking onto it like a suckermouth catfish.

"Oh, fuck, Martez!" she moaned loudly, as he stroked as fast as he could, pushing his nine inches deep into her.

"I'm about to cum Nae," he moaned.

"Pull it out and get it on yo bitch face!"

As the nut traveled closer from his balls, feeling it tingling, Tez snatched his dick from her body and aimed towards her face, stroking hard and fast. The thick, clear substance shot all the way to her forehead. She held her mouth open wide, receiving a good portion on her teeth. He moaned, sounding like an animal, rolling back on the big bed.

"Aht aht. Get yo ass over here and untie me, nigga. We ain't done. It's yo turn," she said, looking around the Air B & B. The room was dark. A small lamp on the dresser by the door gave a little light.

"We gotta take a break, shawty," he said looking around the dark room.

"Ain't no breaks. Untie me!"

He grabbed the small key from the dresser and started uncuffing her.

"Why you keep looking around like that, bae?" she asked.

"I'm just ready to get the fuck out of Georgia. I don't understand why the hell we came back anyway."

"I had to meet with the Miami brokers, bae. I told you that. They're here in Atlanta and said they would be here on business until next month. So my shit could wait a month or I could come meet them myself. You coming back to Florida with me, right?" she asked, stretching out after being fully uncuffed.

"Tonight?" he asked, laying down, allowing her to cuff him.

"Yea," she said, snapping the last cuff on him. She started sucking his soft penis. She licked his balls.

"Woah, hold up, bae! What you doing?" he said, feeling her tongue going between his butt cheeks.

"Trust me. You'll like it," she moaned, stroking her tongue between his crack and stroking his dick.

"Ah, fuck! Hold up, Nae. Man you trippin," he moaned with a serious face.

"Look, baby," she said at how hard his dick had gotten so quickly. "I knew you'd like it," she said before commencing to suck his dick again.

"Hurry up and take these shits off me! You just blowed me!" Tez was irate.

She stopped sucking him and squeezed his dick, turning it.

"Ah, fuck! What the fuck are you doin, shawty?" he screamed. "Uncuff me, now!"

She got up and grabbed her purse off the dresser, returning to her spot in front of him. She pulled out her phone and took a picture of him.

"Nae, un-fuckin-cuff me, now!" he barked, vibrating the room. Nae dressed quickly.

"You stuck the end of your gun," tears dropped quickly. "In my little sister's ass and pulled the trigger." She dropped to her knees crying. "I love you Martez, but I can't let that one go."

"Man, ain do dat shit, shawty! That was Peanut and Smoke!" he snapped, jerking against the restraints. But the thick cherry wood that the cuffs were connected to, wouldn't budge.

"I would love to stick a gun up your ass, but I got something ever better," she cried, not wiping her tears.

"Nae!" Tez hollered as she walked out the room with the handcuff key.

***

"I love you Zaya," Ken said.

"I love you too Kenny," she said, climbing into the bed.

His phone went off. It was a text message from a number he didn't recognize. When he was about to open the text, his phone rung. It was a restricted number calling.

"Please leave that damn phone alone," Zaya whined.

He held up his index finger before answering. "Hello?"

Zaya shook her head and crawled back out of the bed. She slipped into her house shoes and walked out the room.

"As much as I fucking hate you... I got something for you," Nae said.

Ken sat straight up like he was the undertaker. He looked at the phone to make sure he wasn't tripping. His heart sped up.

"Nae," his voice was soft. "You know running from me is only going to last for so long. Please, just give me my son, and I'll let you live freely. I swear," he pleaded.

"You'll never see him again, Ken. Give it up." Her words were slightly cracking.

"Just tell me why," he said, stepping out of bed.

"Why what?" she asked.

"Why the fuck did you start fucking my young nigga, and ran off with him, bitch!" His voice was full of base like a beatbox.

"I started fucking him when you started neglecting me. But how bout we start with me realizing you were lying about who your locked up friend was. You dumb ass nigga. I know you called that hit to get my sister and her boyfriend killed, bitch ass nigga!" She was in a ball of tears. "The reason I ran off with him is because I fell in love with him. The reason you'll never see your son again is because I found that letter, mothafucka!"

"What fuckin' letter?!"

"The letter my dad wrote me saying his roommate is your friend, J-Bo. And after that my dad randomly gets stabbed to fucking death! You took everything from me that I really loved!" She cried, screamed, and kicked.

"Nae, I'm…" he was saying after dropping his head.

"I don't wanna hear it. Check your text messages," she said before hanging up.

***

"We spraying everything moving?" Ty-Ty asked, doing 90 miles per hour on interstate 75 going south.

"I hope so. I'm ready," Snag said from the back seat. J-Bo shot him an evil glare from the rearview mirror.

J-Bo nodded. "Don't let up on dat pedal. I'm tryna get there in half da time," J-Bo said, looking at his GPS, reading three hours until they reach their destination. He looked in the side mirror to see if Jiles and his brother were keeping up. He smiled, seeing that they were right behind him, not lacking.

"Hello?" he answered his ringing phone.

"You got that text message?" Ken asked anxiously.

J-Bo looked at his phone, opening the text. "Who address dat is?" he asked.

"That's where Tez at. He tied to the bed," Ken answered.

"Say less." J-Bo hung up. He dialed for Jiles.

"Hello?" Jiles answered.

"You got dat text?" J-Bo asked.

"I haven't opened it yet, boss. But I got it."

"Okay. Me, Ty-Ty, and Snag got dis. Dat address is where Tez at. Go handle it now," he said before hanging up.

He looked in the side mirror again. Jiles had already switched lanes, preparing to exit the freeway and turn around.

"Asia still ain't tapped in with nobody?" J-Bo asked. Ty-Ty shook his head. Snag looked out the window, then back to J-Bo before saying no. J-Bo grinned.

***

Almost an hour later, the twins pulled up to a big, nice Buckhead house. The neighborhood looked a bit too ghetto. The house didn't really fit in that area, but it was the address J-Bo had given.

"Turn the headlights off, fat boy," Jiles said.

"Shut the fuck up Jiles, please," Kaylin said, killing the engine. He hit the button on the volume knob, and got out the car. They both had to retrieve the pistols under the seat from the outside. They couldn't bend over and do it.

"He said anything bout how we gone get in?" Kaylin asked. Him and his brother strutted up to the house. Once on the porch, Kaylin looked around. Nobody was out.

"He said the door should be open. But even if it's not, I'm sure yo big ass can break in," he laughed. Jiles twisted the knob. It was open.

"We're not separating. We all we got," Kaylin said. His face and voice was serious. Jiles nodded.

"I love you, bra," Kaylin said. He always said that before a mission.

"Love you too, fat boy," Jiles said, smacking his brother's stomach.

There was a flight of stairs as soon as the door opened. Kaylin jogged up, two steps at a time. Jiles was right behind him. Kaylin pulled the 9mm that was hanging from his front pocket once he reached the top of the steps. From where he stood he could see a foot kicking and pulling on the top of the bed. He kneeled all the way down until his eyes were fully adapted to the dark. After about thirty seconds of watching the still air, he knew no one else was there.

"Ah! Fuck! You stupid ass bitch! I'ma kill you hoe! That's on Jesus Christ himself! I'ma get loose and kill you, hoe! Ahh!" Tez hollered at the air from the top of his lungs. "Oh, shit!" He jumped, startled when the twins entered. "Thank God! Fat boys, man, untie me family," he said, breathing so hard his chest moved up and down so far that it seemed almost cartoonish.

Kaylin looked at his brother and they both laughed hard and loud. They walked to different sides of the bed, so one of them was standing on each side of Tez.

"Lil dick ass, lil boy," Jiles said, laughing. Kaylin screamed. He was laughing so hard, his face turned red.

Tez looked back at forth at the twins. "Man, stop playing!" He snatched at the cuffs with all his might.

"You know damn well a nigga ain't finna let you out, Tez. You fucked the big bro wife. Ran off with her. Nigga, you know you finna die tonight," Jiles, said.

"Kaylin… Kay," Tez said. Kaylin turned his head. "Kaylin!" Tez barked through clenched teeth, tears forming in his eyes. "Look at me!"

Kaylin's eyes had formed tears. He looked at Tez.

"Lil bra, I brought you into Young Boss. Listen, at the first chance you can, get out this shit. This shit ain't what it was, family. These niggas don't give a fuck about nobody! This nigga Ken ordered a hit on his own wife's daddy because he ain't want her to find out that he had her lil sista and her sista boyfriend killed," he explained. "This mothafucka J-Bo and his cousin killed a pregnant teenager! And her seventeen years old boyfriend! These niggas don't give a fuck about nobody!" he cried, tears running down his cheeks. "Kaylin, at the end of the day, no matter what I did, I'm yo OG, baby boy. Don't do me like this."

Kaylin wiped the tears from his eyes. "What the hell we gone tell J-Bo if we let you go?" Kaylin asked.

"Oh hell naw! Kaylin, this nigga ain't going nowhere but to his maker tonight," Jiles interrupted.

"Shut up, Jiles!" Kaylin said, throwing some of the blanket on Tez, covering his private area. "This my OG! I can't kill him!"

"Shiiid, he ain't my OG. I bet I can kill his ass," Jiles said, reaching for his pistol.

Kaylin raised his gun on his brother. "Don't do that," Kaylin said.

Jiles slowly moved his hand away from his front pocket where his gun was. "Mothafucka! You gone point a gun at yo own fuckin brother? You gone let this pussy mothafucka trick you? You let this nigga go, he gone get up and kill yo fat ass!" Jiles retorted.

"No, I ain't Kaylin. You know me, lil bra. Kaylin, tell J-Bo when you got here, I was already gone. Listen. I got a million dollars cash. I stole it from Ken before me and shawty took off. It's in that bottom dresser. You can have it all, Kaylin. Just do this one for me, baby boy," Tez said.

"Get it," Kaylin said, still holding his aim on his brother.

"Ain't no fuckin way!" Jiles screamed, snatching the dresser open, pulling the black duffle bag out. He unzipped it. There were stacks of neat bills.

"How I'ma uncuff you?" Kaylin asked.

"She got the keys, and this shit ain't gone budge. You gotta shoot through the wood. Right there," he said once Kaylin aimed at the part of the headboard where the cuffs leaped through. "Shoot it, Kaylin," Tez, said.

"Kaylin, J-Bo not gone believe us!" Jiles yelled.

"Nigga, shut the fuck up. This my OG, I'm not killing him!" Kaylin barked back. "Turn ya head OG."

Tez turned his head, looking at Jiles smiling.

BOOM!

Kaylin pulled the trigger, planting a bullet in Tez's temple. The blood spat up in Kaylin's face. Tez's eyes popped out his head.

Both of the twins laughed. "Got em!" Jiles yelled in Tez's face. They laughed again before running out.

CHAPTER 19

Nae removed a dresser full of underwear, emptying it all into her long suitcase that was on the bed. She speed walked across the room, emptying the next dresser of shirts and socks. She looked at the small, gold Michael Kors watch on her wrist.

"I got time," she whispered, blowing out a deep breath. "About another hour." She power walked into the bathroom, collecting all of her essential face creams. She looked in the mirror and rubbed at the wide bags under her eyes.

Look like somebody beat my ass, she thought, rubbing at the dark circles on her yellow skin. She shook her head, searching for the foundation that fit her skin perfectly. She skipped over the rest of them. They weren't the right color anyway. She loaded them into her bag. Putting her hands on her hips, she looked around the half-furnished room with the queen bed and large dresser and shook her head.

"I actually like it here," she thought aloud, shaking her head. "I was about to deck this place out. It's alright. I'll get that condo in Miami, move the shop there, change the name, and be set."

She sat on the bed when her phone rung. It was Tez's number. She laughed. Dropping the phone back on the bed, she lay back, stretching her arms above her head.

You was wrong for that, Nae. Ken and the guys probably tortured him, she thought, frowning her face as she pictured the gruesome things they probably did to him. *Fuck that bitch ass nigga. He killed my baby*, she thought, going through her phone to find an old picture of her little sister, Diamond. She tried her best to hold it in. Even after a decade, she still couldn't get over it. *Fuck Martez*, she thought.

I should've killed him my damn self. Then I wouldn't have to move. I'm sure he's gonna give them this address in exchange for his freedom, so I'm not chancing it. She pulled the small framed picture of her and her dad at his visitation in prison off the wall. She smiled, rubbing his face. Her eyes watered again. But after batting them a few times, the tears went back to where they came from.

She put that picture inside the luggage. Her phone rung.

"Hey," she answered, sitting back down on the bed.

"Where you at?" he asked.

"Packing my shit. I just decided to leave based off, hypothetically speaking, if somebody was planning on coming here after visiting Tez," she said.

"Get the fuck out of there now. J-Bo is on the way."

She quickly leaped to her feet, and rushed to the light switch, flicking it down. "What? Why are you just now telling me this?" She went to the window scanning the parking lot. The six vehicles, including her own, were all familiar.

"I just found out. Get the hell out of there, now. Call me when you get to where you going. You gotta ditch yo car and get an Uber, or something," he said.

"Shit! Okay!" She hung up, rushing back to the bed. She zipped the suitcase closed, slid it off the bed, pulled the handle up and rolled it to the front door.

***

"Don't park in front of the buildin', fam. Go over one," J-Bo said, looking at the address on the postcard as Ty-Ty turned into the Live Oak apartment complex.

"Which one is it?" Ty-Ty asked, leaning closer to the windshield, trying to read the letters on the building through the dark night.

"Dis shit say D-16…" J-Bo said, looking up. "So, A, B, C, D… stop in front of da second buildin'."

Ty-Ty stopped. J-Bo got out and jogged to the building. Looking up, there was a letter B at the top. He jogged back to the car.

"Yea, park here. Dis B, so dat gotta be D." He pointed two buildings down.

"We ain't tryna kill her here," J-Bo said, looking at Ty-Ty. He looked in the backseat to Snag. "We tryna snatch her, and get her back to da city. I want Ken to witness it," he said.

Ty-Ty and Snag, nodded their understandings.

"If she transgress or pose a threat?" Ty-Ty asked.

"What you thank, nigga? Pop that hoe too," Snag spat.

"Man shut da f..." Ty-Ty was saying.

"Respect rank, nigga!" Snag punched the back of Ty-Ty's seat.

J-Bo gave both of them a firm stare like a mother does her child before whooping their ass. "If you say jump, and dis bitch does anything but jump... pop her," J-Bo said, hitting the button on the volume knob. Everyone grabbed their pistols. "Ain got time for nobody dying' or gettin' hurt tonight; at least not one of us."

They nodded.

"Hold up," J-Bo said. He dialed a number, put the phone to his ear, then put it back in the ashtray holder.

"Asia ain't hit nan one of y'all?," He frowned.

Ty-Ty and Snag both said no, trying to call her.

"Straight to voicemail," Snag said.

"Same," Ty-Ty said.

"Fuck! I hope she aight. We gotta do a serious investigation after dis, because she had just hit me, saying she was on her way. She had to tell me sum important. I'm a tell y'all dis now. If she don't pop up by da time we get back, we sprayin' Squeek shit."

"You talkin' about the dike from Campbellton?" Ty-Ty asked.

"Yea," J-Bo answered.

"Why her spot?" he asked.

"Because dat's da last place I known her to be... Come on, let's rock," J-Bo said, getting out the truck.

The buildings were long and seemed to never separate. They were all connected by the sides. The three men dressed in all black jumpsuits ran towards the building, getting so close that the creases of their shirts were running against the red brick building. They ran through short bushes, and mud puddles, then stopped, hearing a noise. J-Bo pulled his 9mm, and quickly peaked around the corner. He held his open palm to Ty-Ty and Snag, whom was behind him. Peaking around the corner, it was an elderly man coming out of his apartment. J-Bo looked up. The building read: C.

They stood beside the building as the older man entered his car. They were blended with the dark night and dark clothes. J-Bo dropped to his knees once the older man got to his car and the other two men followed suit. When they squatted, they were behind a thick bush, hiding them from the old man's headlights. Once he pulled off J-Bo took off again; Snag and Ty-Ty on his heels. After another set of bushes and mud puddles, they were at the next building. Looking up, he saw the letter D on the building. He peaked around the corner swiftly. Seeing no one, he ran around the corner. There was a two layered breezeway: one downstairs, one upstairs.

He ran around the corner with his weapon drawn. There were eight apartments on the bottom tier. He ran quietly to all of them reading the door numbers. D1… D2… D3… D4… D5… D6… D7… D8…

Gotta be upstairs, he thought. He skipped the first few apartments. Just judging from the way the bottom was set-up, he knew 16 had to be the last apartment on the top. Once in front of D16, he looked back to the guys.

"On three," he whispered. Ty-Ty nodded. Snag stopped to the left side of Ty-Ty and aimed his gun at the door.

"This looks like thick metal," Ty-Ty whispered, judging the door.

"If dis bitch don't open in one kick, Snag shoot the lock, shawty," J-Bo said.

Snag nodded.

"One, two..." J-Bo said positioning himself.

***

At the front door, just when Nae was about to twist the lock she remembered something. She ran back to the room, into the bathroom, reaching under the cabinet.

Can't forget these, she thought, pulling a bag of tampons out. She ran to the front door, stuck them down in her bag, and stood. While reaching for the knob, something felt odd. She looked back at the balcony, then back to the door.

Fuck that shit girl. Just get out of here, she thought.

She placed her hand on the doorknob, preparing to turn it. It wouldn't turn.

Damn, I'm nervous. I forgot to unlock the mothafucka, she thought.

***

"Three!" J-Bo yelled. He and Ty-Ty's foot crashed into the lock. The door pushed in a little, but didn't fall. They both stepped to the side, and Snag sent two shots at the lock. The lock fell and the door slung open. Ty-Ty kicked it again, the door fell in and he and J-Bo rushed in. The blinds from the balcony were moving.

"Balcony!" J-Bo yelled.

Snag ran down the flight of steps and around the building. By the time he spent the corner, Nae was jumping up from the ground and running. Snag stood still and took aim. He pulled the trigger as she was just turning the corner.

Fuck, he thought.

J-Bo and Ty-Ty ran out towards Snag.

"Go that way!" Snag screamed, pointing towards the front of the building. He ran towards the way where he shot at. Ty-Ty and J-Bo ran the other way.

In the front of the building, Nae ran straight into Ty-Ty's arms. She yelled at the top of her lungs; an ear-piercing sound. Ty-Ty let her go. She ran again.

"The fuck you let her go for, nigga?" Snag questioned, aiming at Nae. It seemed like as soon as he pulled the trigger, she dropped, rolled, got back up and started running.

J-Bo pushed Snag. "Stop fuckin shootin, nigga!"

Ty-Ty hopped in the truck, not wanting to be seen by the few apartment lights that came on after the gunshots. J-Bo and Ty-Ty gave chase on foot. Turning the corner, Ty-Ty saw her and could've easily hit her. But he drove past, stopping in front of a parked car at the complex entrance, just when Nae was getting in the back of that car.

"Let her out," J-Bo said, stretching his arm through the driver side window, scratching his gun against the young man's beard.

***

"Want me to call Ken, boss?" Ty-Ty asked, driving back to Atlanta. Nae was in the backseat between J-Bo and Snag.

"Nah, I'll hit him in a second," he said, snatching Nae's phone from her breast. The screen was already unlocked. He went to the recent call log and the name he saw made his jaw drop...

What the fuck? So yo pussy ass been protecting these mothafuckas, he thought.

CHAPTER 20

The rest of the ride was silent. J-Bo couldn't believe what his eyes had seen.

Dat's da typa shit these mothafuckas really got goin on? Really? He thought over and over, trying not to believe it. He shook his head, and pulled out his own phone, giving Ken a call to update him on what was what.

"I'm on my way back to Atlanta. Save her for me," he said.

J-Bo promised him he would and got off the phone. He gave Smoke a call. Smoke said he still hadn't heard from Asia or seen her. Smoke said he'd been out all day and night looking for her, and was ready to go and wet Squeek shit up. J-Bo told him to wait, so they could give Squeek and them a proper war proposal: either produce Asia, or war with Young Boss. Smoke didn't really like the idea. He wanted to pop on them folks ASAP, but he respected J-Bo's word.

***

Asia almost dozed off lying on them steps, pretending to be knocked out, or dead. She got up at hearing Lameka's shallow moans from under her. Again she scooted all the way down the steps. "Lameka, shh!" she whispered. She rolled Lameka from her side again to her back. Her eyes fluttered before finally opening.

"Lameka, this is Asia." She waved her hand in front of Lameka's face. "I need you to wake all the way up for me, okay?" She gently slapped Lameka's face.

"Asia, where are we?" Lameka asked. She tried to sit up and shot backwards in pain, clutching her private area.

"Oww," she moaned.

Asia shed a tear, assuming she knew what Lameka's issue was.

"It's okay, Lameka. Get up. Let's try and get the fuck out of here," she said, wiping sweat and tears from her face. Asia kept wiping and slapping at her arm every time the pigs made noise.

Feel like shit keeps crawling on me, she thought, scratching deep into her skin.

"Lameka! Get yo ass up or you gone get left," she said, anxiously pulling at Lameka's arm.

"Umm," Lameka moaned.

This bitch must've been drugged or something, Asia thought. She let Lameka's arm go and ran to the steel cabinet. Right when she stood in front of the cabinet, she heard footsteps above her; and a voice, the same one from earlier. She pulled the handle up and down with all her might. It wouldn't budge. She looked around the dark room for something, anything. She ran to the corner, seeing a raggedy toolbox. Flipping the top open, there were a few Phillip headed screwdrivers and a long wrench. She grabbed the wrench, and ran back to the cabinet.

This shit heavier than it looks, she thought, raising the wrench with both of her hands.

Wait! Don't hit it hard… Fuck that. That nigga said he keeps some guns down here. I've looked everywhere so it gotta be in here. But what if it's not? Then we just in trouble. I'll have to use this wrench, she thought, slamming the wrench into the metal handle. The handle broke off and fell straight to the floor. She dropped the wrench and opened the two doors.

"Oh shit," she barely whispered.

There was an arsenal of handguns sitting on a short metal shelf. She skimmed through the guns quickly, looking for the one she was familiar with. Seeing a black and silver 9mm, she quickly snatched it up.

Where the fuck is the bullets? she thought, opening a drawer on the shelf. She quickly smiled and stopped looking for bullets. She remembered J-Bo telling her to know the difference between a gun that's loaded and one that's not. She knew it was loaded from the weight. She released the clip just to see. It was. She slapped it back into the gun, cocked the head back, and ran back over to Lameka.

The footsteps seemed heavier and more rapid from upstairs. She aimed upwards and started walking up slowly. Once she hit the third step the door swung open. She fired.

Pop! Pop! Pop!

A body dropped. Lameka and jumped up screaming.

"Be quiet, Meka. We're okay," Asia snapped, still staring up the stairs. The body fell at the top of the steps and started slowly rolling over the top steps, as the man's weight hung. Once over the top steps the body rolled all the way down the steps. Lameka ran to the side. Asia stepped back a foot, but held her aim upstairs at the door opening.

"You ready to go?" Asia said, finally breaking her visual from the door to Lameka. Lameka had her hands covering her ears. She nodded.

Asia stepped over the man. She used her shoe to push his head over so she could see him.

What the fuck, she thought, staring at the older man's face. Where the fuck do I know you from? Oh, shit! This is the man that let us practice our shooting on his property. What the fuck? So did J-Bo and Ty-Ty know about this too? she wondered.

"Come on, Meka," she said, pointing the gun up, taking the steps two at a time. Lameka was on her heels. Through the door she was in the kitchen. Everything was wooden. The smell of farm animals and manure invaded her nostrils. It was the same odor she smelled when they originally came to the farm for her to learn how to shoot. She quickly identified a set of keys on the wooden table. She pocketed them, and turned her gun around the corner. She grabbed Lameka by the hand and they ran through the spacious farmhouse. Once on the front porch, she stood there, looking around the pitch black night. She ran to the white pick-up truck and unlocked the door. She got in and started the engine. Lameka climbed in the passenger.

"I'll be right back," Asia said, running back into the house.

"Where you going!" Lameka screamed, looking around frantically.

Asia ran into the house and back into the basement. He was still there. She ran down the steps and looked to the right. She smiled, seeing the two wooden tables.

That's why those damn tables looked so familiar. Those the tables we were shooting on, she thought.

She ran over to the door where the pigs were making all kinds of crazy noises.

"You old mothafuckas was gon feed us to some fucking pigs," she said, shedding another tear. "Well, it's never fun when the rabbit gets the fucking gun," she thought aloud, twisting the knob. She pushed the door wide open and took off running, skipping up the steps. The pigs instantly came running out behind her. She looked back at the top of the steps and the three animals were hungrily eating at the old man's flesh. Their teeth easily tore through his old skin and bone fragments. She turned, running back to the truck where Lameka was.

CHAPTER 21

"I'm in. How far away is Ken?" Ty-Ty asked, pulling up in front of the warehouse.

"He took a private flight, so he should be here soon," J-Bo said, looking at his phone. "And nobody ain't heard from Asia yet?" he asked, dialing her number again. Voicemail.

Ty-Ty looked at his phone. "My shit dead."

"Hell naw. She still ain't called me," Snag said.

J-Bo looked at both of them for a few seconds, then back to his phone, dialing for her again to no avail.

"Wassup wit Asia? She been givin you da heads up, bitch?" J-Bo asked Nae, aggressively squeezing her neck as he stepped out the truck, pulling her along.

"No!" She cried.

He had one hand around her neck, and one tangled in her hair. He pulled her towards the building. Ty-Ty and Snag got out next. Ty-Ty unlocked the door. They all entered.

"Throw me dat chair," J-Bo said, pointing up.

Snag ran upstairs, grabbed one of the chairs, and threw it down over the top range. Ty-Ty caught it, and put it down. J-Bo slung Nae on it.

"You gon' tape her hands, fam?" Snag asked from the top range, about to go to where he knew some tape was.

"Hell naw. If dis bitch move, I'ma shoot her," J-Bo said, looking at his phone, dialing for Smoke.

"Any word on Asia?" he asked when Smoke answered.

"Not yet," he answered.

"Hurry up! Get to da warehouse. I need erbody in attendance," he said, hanging up.

J-Bo had already texted the twins, telling them to be there to escort Ken from his private charter destination to the warehouse. They were there to pick him up.

"What's going on?" Ken asked, getting in the truck. Jiles walked behind him with his gun out.

"We got Tez and Nae," Kaylin said, stepping on the gas as soon as Ken closed his door. He stopped, remembering Jiles. Once Jiles climbed in, he stepped on the gas again. Jiles handed Ken a small bag.

"What's this?" he asked.

"Tez had it. He said it's a million. Say he stole it from you before him and ol' girl ran off," he explained.

Ken handed the bag back. "Y'all can split it. Just get me to these mother fuckers," he said.

"I'm taking you to her, big bra," Kaylin said.

"What about Tez?" he asked.

"I kilt him," Kaylin said.

The twins and Smoke were arriving at the warehouse around the same time.

"What you doing out in the wee hours, big bra? You know we will handle all the business," Smoke said, giving Ken dap.

"Some things are personal, little brother," Ken said, power walking from the truck in his dark gray pajama set. The twins and Smoke followed him in. When Nae saw him she instantly puked on the floor in the space in front of her.

"Oh, now you want to throw up, bitch?" Ken said, approaching her aggressively. He open palm smacked her as hard as he could. Her bright skin reddened quickly, and she fell from the chair to the ground on her bottom.

"You bitch!" Ken screamed, smacking her again across the face, sending her flat on her back. He stood over her with a balled-up fist. "Why?!" he screamed, tears rolling down his face.

"I told you why, Ken. You killed my…"

He cut her off with another smack. This time it was a backhand. The force busted her lip and swelled her left eye.

"The fuck you take me for? Sam Sausage Head?! You been fuckin' this nigga. This ain't nothin' fresh. I don't know exactly how long, but it's been a while. Maybe even years.

And yo sister was a snitch ass bitch! I tried to reason with her. She took the money and still testified. What part of the game is that? What was I supposed to do, huh?! She's the reason my people did ten years in prison. I was never supposed to fall in love with you. It was never the fucking plan! But I did. And I gave your bitch ass the fucking world!" He smacked her again. "I hate you, bitch!" He smacked her again, knocking her unconscious. He stretched his arms out.

"J-Bo, see if this bitch is dead," Ken said, cracking his knuckles.

J-Bo ran over to her and jammed two fingers into her throat, feeling for a pulse.

"She alive, big bra," J-Bo said.

Ken stood over her and smacked her again. This time it was harder than all the other times, waking her back up.

"Where the fuck is my son?!" Ken wolfed.

Nae looked up at him through fluttery, bleeding eyes.

"You will never see him again, nigga," she whispered slowly through a pair of bleeding lips. She glanced at Smoke.

"J-Bo, give me a fucking gun. I'm gonna kill this bitch!" Ken barked.

***

Asia stepped on the gas pedal, not knowing exactly how to get out of that country ass part of Georgia. She followed all main streets, hoping to find a highway. She was sure to avoid all back roads.

"Meka, you okay?" she asked, glancing at Lameka.

Lameka was in the passenger seat, silently clutching her private area.

"Yes. I just want to go home." She began to cry. "I don't give a damn about that money Asia. You can keep it. Please just take me home."

Asia nodded. "I promise you, you're going home, baby. And you getting the money. But I need you to talk to J-Bo immediately," she said, pressing harder on the pedal trying to go faster. Asia smiled hard, seeing a highway going north. She quickly switched lanes without using turning signals. She searched the truck for a cellphone. There was none. She checked the glove compartment. There was none.

"Fuck!" She screamed, giving herself a headache all over again. Fifteen minutes later, she came off on the exit closet to where J-Bo was staying. She pulled in front of Shakeena's house. She blew the horn several times before jumping out of the truck and banging on the door.

***

Ken stared Nae down for a good fifteen minutes straight. She was on the ground with him standing over her with his gun in her face.

"Nae, I swear this is my last time asking you. Where the fuck is my son?" he spat, tears still running from his eyes.

"I'm going to be honest with you, Ken." She swallowed a gulp of spit and blood.

J-Bo's phone rung. He ignored it. It rung again.

"J-Bo, shut the fucking phone off!" Ken snapped.

Just when he was about to power the phone off, he decided to read the text message from Shakeena.

She's usually sleep so this might be an emergency, he thought. The text message read: ASIA IS HERE. SHE LOOKS BAD. SHE'S ASKING WHERE ARE YOU???

He quickly texted back, telling her his whereabouts.

"J-Bo how you think I should handle this bitch?" He threw his head back with enough force to whip his dreads to the back of his head.

"I say you tie her up, right here. Feed her ass a bolony sandwich every day and leave her like dat until you get ova her sucka ass betrayal mentally. Den when you over it, I'll politely come in here and kill da bitch," J-Bo suggested.

Ken smiled, rubbing his wild beard. He turned to the twins. "What about y'all?"

"I say we get a bunch of crackheads and let them take they time fuckin' her. Then we kill her," Kaylin said, laughing hard. Jiles laughed with him.

Ken looked at the twins like they were crazy before smiling hard. "Y'all niggas are crazy. I like both ideas."

Ken looked at Smoke and noticed he was making eye contact with Nae. They quickly broke contact when they noticed Ken was looking.

"What the hell you staring at my young boy for bitch?" Ken asked, kicking Nae in the side.

There was loud banging at the door. Everybody trained their guns to the sound.

"It's cool y'all! Chill. Open da doe, Kaylin," J-Bo said.

Everybody looked at J-Bo like he was crazy.

"You ordered pizza or something?" Kaylin asked, looking at his twin brother. They both laughed.

"Open da damn doe!" J-Bo snapped.

Kaylin opened the door and Asia came walking in followed by Lameka.

"What the hell happened to you?" Ken asked, looking at all of the dried blood on Asia's face and arms. "And who is she?" he asked, eyeing Lameka.

The second Asia stepped foot past Kaylin, Snag commenced to raise his gun, taking aim on her. She beat him to the punch by dropping to her butt and shooting him in the shoulder. He dropped his gun and screamed.

"Ah! Kill that bitch!" Snag screamed, squeezing his shoulder, blood flowing through his fingers.

Everybody in attendance raised their weapons on Asia.

"You better have a good ass reason why you did that, or your dying tonight," Ken said calmly.

"When I called you J-Bo, and told you I was on the way, this nigga." She pointed her gun at Snag. "Ran me off the fucking road and raped her!" She nodded to Lameka. "And took us to the fucking farm where you taught me how to shoot, to be eatin by some fucking pigs!" she spat.

"I don't believe that shit. Why the fuck would he do that?" Kaylin said, ready for the word to kill Asia.

"She lying!" Snag yelled.

"Why would he do that, huh?" Asia asked, looking back. "You see this girl right here holding her pussy, crying and shit. Snag raped her!"

"She lyin. Kill that hoe!" Snag screamed.

"You gotta make it make sense, Asia," J-Bo said.

Asia looked back to Lameka. "When I called J-Bo, and said I was on the way, what was I coming to tell him?"

Lameka sniffled hard. "The two people that Snag killed were my cousins. He made up a bullshit ass story about he gonna pay them a hundred thousand dollars to change their names. Once they changed their names, he told them to meet him in the Bluff and he killed them," Lameka explained.

"That's why he did it, so that wouldn't get out. What's the fucking odds of him killing them like that? Why the fuck would they be freely rolling around the Bluff, knowing they're in trouble?" She crossed her arms.

J-Bo looked at Ken. "How else would she know bout da pigs?"

Ken shrugged his shoulders. J-Bo shot Snag between the eyes, killing him.

"What you gone do with dis bitch, big bra?" J-Bo asked.

"You gone tell me where my son at?" Ken asked her.

"I swear. I don't…" She was saying until another one of Ken's forceful smacks sent her unconscious again. "Kaylin and Jiles, y'all handle this," Ken said, nodding to Snag's body. "Tie this bitch up with his dead body and let her sit with him until she die, too!"

The twins nodded.

"One thing, though, two things fasho…this warehouse is the end of the road for you. If you want our son to grow up fatherless without my resources and a decent shot at life, so be it!"

"I got sum to say." J-Bo stepped up to Asia's side.

"You got loyalty to dis organization, shawty?" J-Bo asked.

"You fuckin right I do! All this shit I been through." She shed a tear.

"And anybody tryna come against or between us or bring betrayal on us, you willing to kill em in cold blood?" J-Bo asked.

Asia nodded. "You fuckin right!" Asia said with confidence.

"Meka, shawty, you might wanna leave, unless you tryna be the next female to join Young Boss," J-Bo said.

"Yea, I'll just go…," she was saying.

"Bitch, you bet not go nowhere. You Young Boss, now!" Asia wolfed, staring at Lameka through teary eyes. Lameka stood there.

Ken smiled at J-Bo.

J-Bo looked at Asia. "Young Boss, Young Boss, 25-2 I'll neva cross," J-Bo said. She recited it after him.

"I hate to put you in a position like this but I need to know where yo loyalty at," he said.

"Huh?" She twisted her face.

"What the fuck going on, J-Bo?" Ken asked.

"Asia, kill Smoke now. He's the one that's been giving Nae and Tez all them tips, letting dem know what we was up to. When we ran in on her, she was in a big rush leaving through the fucking balcony. I finally got her phone, and she was talkin' to Smoke minutes before. Kill him now, or I'ma thank you was helpin dem too, shawty," J-Bo said.

Ken's eyes grew wide and he looked to Smoke. "Is this…true?"

Smoke dropped his head. "I worked for my rank for like a decade, bra. That shit hurt me so bad when y'all took it away from me and gave rank to my girl…" Smoke was explaining.

"Kill him or I'ma kill you!" J-Bo snapped.

Tears flowed heavily from Asia's eyes as she raised the gun, and took aim at Smoke's heart. She was torn. A part of her understood where he was coming from. Ten years was a long time and a huge chunk of your life to dedicate to a cause only to be stripped of everything you worked so hard for. And the fact that he had only been following the orders of his superior, made it all the more unfair. Despite the fact, her gun was raised.

She came in the game with simple ideals, but she had to adapt. The world was not a simple place. If not before she joined Young Boss, it was clear to her now that the same set of rules didn't apply to everyone. So no, life wasn't fair, but at some point, you had to decide if that was something you could live with. Asia's mind was made up.

Smoke stared back at her with his chin high. "I'm still a boss."

"Now!" J-Bo yelled.

Without a second thought, Asia pulled the trigger, and planted a bullet in Smoke's heart, sending him back to the floor in a heap with his eyes open, staring at nothing. The spot of blood that stained his shirt grew as he laid there lifeless.

"All disloyalty gets dealt with," Ken said, running from the warehouse followed by everyone else.

The twins stayed to clean up the mess.

THE END

Lock Down Publications and Ca$h Presents
Assisted Publishing Packages

BASIC PACKAGE	UPGRADED PACKAGE
$499	$800
Editing	Typing
Cover Design	Editing
Formatting	Cover Design
	Formatting
ADVANCE PACKAGE	**LDP SUPREME PACKAGE**
$1,200	$1,500
Typing	Typing
Editing	Editing
Cover Design	Cover Design
Formatting	Formatting
Copyright registration	Copyright registration
Proofreading	Proofreading
Upload book to Amazon	Set up Amazon account
	Upload book to Amazon
	Advertise on LDP, Amazon and Facebook Page

***Other services available upon request.
Additional charges may apply
Lock Down Publications
P.O. Box 944
Stockbridge, GA 30281-9998
Phone: 470 303-9761

Submission Guideline

Submit the first three chapters of your completed manuscript to ldpsubmissions@gmail.com, subject line: Your book's title. The manuscript must be in a .doc file and sent as an attachment. Document should be in Times New Roman, double spaced and in size 12 font. Also, provide your synopsis and full contact information. If sending multiple submissions, they must each be in a separate email.

Have a story but no way to send it electronically? You can still submit to LDP/Ca$h Presents. Send in the first three chapters, written or typed, of your completed manuscript to:

LDP: Submissions Dept
Po Box 944
Stockbridge, Ga 30281

DO NOT send original manuscript. Must be a duplicate.

Provide your synopsis and a cover letter containing your full contact information.

Thanks for considering LDP and Ca$h Presents.

NEW RELEASES

BLOODLINE OF A SAVAGE
BY PRINCE A. TAUHID
THE MURDER QUEENS 4
BY MICHAEL GALLON
THE BUTTERFLY MAFIA
BY FUMIYA PAYNE
KING KILLA 2
BY VINCENT "VITTO" HOLLOWAY
BABY, I'M WINTERTIME COLD 3
BY MEESHA
THESE VICIOUS STREETS
BY PRINCE A. TAUHID
TIL DEATH 2
BY ARYANNA
CITY OF SMOKE 2
BY MOLOTTI
PRODUCT OF THE STREETS
BY DEMOND "MONEY" ANDERSON
STEPPERS
BY KING RIO
THE LANE
BY KEN-KEN SPENCE
MONEY GAME 2
BY SMOOVE DOLLA
THE BLACK DIAMOND CARTEL
BY SAYNOMORE
CRIME BOSS 2
BY PLAYA RAY
THE BIRTH OF A GANGSTER 4
BY DELMONT PLAYER
THUG OF SPADES
BY COREY ROBINSON
LOVE IN THE TRENCHES 2
BY COREY ROBINSON
TIL DEATH 3
BY ARYANNA

Available Now

BLOOD OF A BOSS **VI**
SHADOWS OF THE GAME II
TRAP BASTARD II
By Askari
LOYAL TO THE GAME **IV**
By T.J. & Jelissa
TRUE SAVAGE **VIII**
MIDNIGHT CARTEL IV
DOPE BOY MAGIC IV
CITY OF KINGZ III
NIGHTMARE ON SILENT AVE II
THE PLUG OF LIL MEXICO II
CLASSIC CITY II
By Chris Green
BLAST FOR ME **III**
A SAVAGE DOPEBOY III
CUTTHROAT MAFIA III
DUFFLE BAG CARTEL VII
HEARTLESS GOON VI
By Ghost
A HUSTLER'S DECEIT III
KILL ZONE II
BAE BELONGS TO ME III
TIL DEATH II
By Aryanna
KING OF THE TRAP III
By T.J. Edwards
GORILLAZ IN THE BAY V
3X KRAZY III
STRAIGHT BEAST MODE III
De'Kari
KINGPIN KILLAZ IV

STREET KINGS III
PAID IN BLOOD III
CARTEL KILLAZ IV
DOPE GODS III
Hood Rich
SINS OF A HUSTLA II
ASAD
YAYO V
Bred In The Game 2
S. Allen
THE STREETS WILL TALK II
By Yolanda Moore
SON OF A DOPE FIEND III
HEAVEN GOT A GHETTO III
SKI MASK MONEY III
By Renta
LOYALTY AIN'T PROMISED III
By Keith Williams
I'M NOTHING WITHOUT HIS LOVE II
SINS OF A THUG II
TO THE THUG I LOVED BEFORE II
IN A HUSTLER I TRUST II
By Monet Dragun
QUIET MONEY IV
EXTENDED CLIP III
THUG LIFE IV
By Trai'Quan
THE STREETS MADE ME IV
By Larry D. Wright
IF YOU CROSS ME ONCE III
ANGEL V
By Anthony Fields
THE STREETS WILL NEVER CLOSE IV
By K'ajji
HARD AND RUTHLESS III

KILLA KOUNTY IV
By Khufu
MONEY GAME III
By Smoove Dolla
JACK BOYS VS DOPE BOYS IV
A GANGSTA'S QUR'AN V
COKE GIRLZ II
COKE BOYS II
LIFE OF A SAVAGE V
CHI'RAQ GANGSTAS V
SOSA GANG III
BRONX SAVAGES II
BODYMORE KINGPINS II
By Romell Tukes
MURDA WAS THE CASE III
Elijah R. Freeman
AN UNFORESEEN LOVE IV
BABY, I'M WINTERTIME COLD III
By Meesha

QUEEN OF THE ZOO III
By Black Migo
CONFESSIONS OF A JACKBOY III
By Nicholas Lock
KING KILLA II
By Vincent "Vitto" Holloway
BETRAYAL OF A THUG III
By Fre$h
THE MURDER QUEENS III
By Michael Gallon
THE BIRTH OF A GANGSTER III
By Delmont Player
TREAL LOVE II
By Le'Monica Jackson
FOR THE LOVE OF BLOOD III

By Jamel Mitchell
RAN OFF ON DA PLUG II
By Paper Boi Rari
HOOD CONSIGLIERE III
By Keese
PRETTY GIRLS DO NASTY THINGS II
By Nicole Goosby
PROTÉGÉ OF A LEGEND III
LOVE IN THE TRENCHES II
By Corey Robinson
IT'S JUST ME AND YOU II
By Ah'Million
FOREVER GANGSTA III
By Adrian Dulan
GORILLAZ IN THE TRENCHES II
By SayNoMore
THE COCAINE PRINCESS VIII
By King Rio
CRIME BOSS II
Playa Ray
LOYALTY IS EVERYTHING III
Molotti
HERE TODAY GONE TOMORROW II
By Fly Rock
REAL G'S MOVE IN SILENCE II
By Von Diesel
GRIMEY WAYS IV
By Ray Vinci
RESTRAINING ORDER **I & II**
By CA$H & Coffee
LOVE KNOWS NO BOUNDARIES **I II & III**
By Coffee
RAISED AS A GOON I, II, III & IV
BRED BY THE SLUMS I, II, III
BLAST FOR ME I & II

ROTTEN TO THE CORE I II III
A BRONX TALE I, II, III
DUFFLE BAG CARTEL I II III IV V VI
HEARTLESS GOON I II III IV V
A SAVAGE DOPEBOY I II
DRUG LORDS I II III
CUTTHROAT MAFIA I II
KING OF THE TRENCHES
By Ghost
LAY IT DOWN **I & II**
LAST OF A DYING BREED I II
BLOOD STAINS OF A SHOTTA I & II III
By Jamaica
LOYAL TO THE GAME I II III
LIFE OF SIN I, II III
By TJ & Jelissa
BLOODY COMMAS I & II
SKI MASK CARTEL I II & III
KING OF NEW YORK I II,III IV V
RISE TO POWER I II III
COKE KINGS I II III IV V
BORN HEARTLESS I II III IV
KING OF THE TRAP I II
By T.J. Edwards
IF LOVING HIM IS WRONG…I & II
LOVE ME EVEN WHEN IT HURTS I II III
By Jelissa
WHEN THE STREETS CLAP BACK I & II III
THE HEART OF A SAVAGE I II III IV
MONEY MAFIA I II
LOYAL TO THE SOIL I II III
By Jibril Williams
A DISTINGUISHED THUG STOLE MY HEART I II & III
LOVE SHOULDN'T HURT I II III IV
RENEGADE BOYS I II III IV

PAID IN KARMA I II III
SAVAGE STORMS I II III
AN UNFORESEEN LOVE I II III
BABY, I'M WINTERTIME COLD I II
By Meesha
A GANGSTER'S CODE I &, II III
A GANGSTER'S SYN I II III
THE SAVAGE LIFE I II III
CHAINED TO THE STREETS I II III
BLOOD ON THE MONEY I II III
A GANGSTA'S PAIN I II III
By J-Blunt
PUSH IT TO THE LIMIT
By Bre' Hayes
BLOOD OF A BOSS I, II, III, IV, V
SHADOWS OF THE GAME
TRAP BASTARD
By Askari
THE STREETS BLEED MURDER **I, II & III**
THE HEART OF A GANGSTA I II& III
By Jerry Jackson
CUM FOR ME I II III IV V VI VII VIII
An LDP Erotica Collaboration
BRIDE OF A HUSTLA **I II & II**
THE FETTI GIRLS **I, II& III**
CORRUPTED BY A GANGSTA I, II III, IV
BLINDED BY HIS LOVE
THE PRICE YOU PAY FOR LOVE I, II ,III
DOPE GIRL MAGIC I II III
By Destiny Skai
WHEN A GOOD GIRL GOES BAD
By Adrienne
THE COST OF LOYALTY I II III
By Kweli
A GANGSTER'S REVENGE **I II III & IV**

THE BOSS MAN'S DAUGHTERS I II III IV V
A SAVAGE LOVE **I & II**
BAE BELONGS TO ME I II
A HUSTLER'S DECEIT I, II, III
WHAT BAD BITCHES DO I, II, III
SOUL OF A MONSTER I II III
KILL ZONE
A DOPE BOY'S QUEEN I II III
TIL DEATH
By Aryanna
A KINGPIN'S AMBITON
A KINGPIN'S AMBITION **II**
I MURDER FOR THE DOUGH
By Ambitious
TRUE SAVAGE I II III IV V VI VII
DOPE BOY MAGIC I, II, III
MIDNIGHT CARTEL I II III
CITY OF KINGZ I II
NIGHTMARE ON SILENT AVE
THE PLUG OF LIL MEXICO II
CLASSIC CITY
By Chris Green
A DOPEBOY'S PRAYER
By Eddie "Wolf" Lee
THE KING CARTEL **I, II & III**
By Frank Gresham
THESE NIGGAS AIN'T LOYAL **I, II & III**
By Nikki Tee
GANGSTA SHYT **I II &III**
By CATO
THE ULTIMATE BETRAYAL
By Phoenix
Boss'n Up i , ii & IIi
By Royal Nicole
I LOVE YOU TO DEATH

By Destiny J
I RIDE FOR MY HITTA
I STILL RIDE FOR MY HITTA
By Misty Holt
LOVE & CHASIN' PAPER
By Qay Crockett
TO DIE IN VAIN
SINS OF A HUSTLA
By ASAD
BROOKLYN HUSTLAZ
By Boogsy Morina
BROOKLYN ON LOCK I & II
By Sonovia
GANGSTA CITY
By Teddy Duke
A DRUG KING AND HIS DIAMOND I & II III
A DOPEMAN'S RICHES
HER MAN, MINE'S TOO I, II
CASH MONEY HO'S
THE WIFEY I USED TO BE I II
PRETTY GIRLS DO NASTY THINGS
By Nicole Goosby
TRAPHOUSE KING **I II & III**
KINGPIN KILLAZ I II III
STREET KINGS I II
PAID IN BLOOD **I II**
CARTEL KILLAZ I II III
DOPE GODS I II
By Hood Rich
LIPSTICK KILLAH **I, II, III**
CRIME OF PASSION I II & III
FRIEND OR FOE I II III
By Mimi
STEADY MOBBN' **I, II, III**
THE STREETS STAINED MY SOUL I II III

By Marcellus Allen
WHO SHOT YA **I, II, III**
SON OF A DOPE FIEND I II
HEAVEN GOT A GHETTO I II
SKI MASK MONEY I II
Renta
GORILLAZ IN THE BAY **I II III IV**
TEARS OF A GANGSTA I II
3X KRAZY I II
STRAIGHT BEAST MODE I II
DE'KARI
TRIGGADALE I II III
MURDAROBER WAS THE CASE I II
Elijah R. Freeman
GOD BLESS THE TRAPPERS I, II, III
THESE SCANDALOUS STREETS I, II, III
FEAR MY GANGSTA I, II, III IV, V
THESE STREETS DON'T LOVE NOBODY I, II
BURY ME A G I, II, III, IV, V
A GANGSTA'S EMPIRE I, II, III, IV
THE DOPEMAN'S BODYGAURD I II
THE REALEST KILLAZ I II III
THE LAST OF THE OGS I II III
Tranay Adams
THE STREETS ARE CALLING
Duquie Wilson
MARRIED TO A BOSS I II III
By Destiny Skai & Chris Green
KINGZ OF THE GAME I II III IV V VI VII
CRIME BOSS
Playa Ray
SLAUGHTER GANG I II III
RUTHLESS HEART I II III
By Willie Slaughter
FUK SHYT

By Blakk Diamond
DON'T F#CK WITH MY HEART I II
By Linnea
ADDICTED TO THE DRAMA I II III
IN THE ARM OF HIS BOSS II
By Jamila
YAYO I II III IV
A SHOOTER'S AMBITION I II
BRED IN THE GAME
By S. Allen
TRAP GOD I II III
RICH $AVAGE I II III
MONEY IN THE GRAVE I II III
By Martell Troublesome Bolden
FOREVER GANGSTA I II
GLOCKS ON SATIN SHEETS I II
By Adrian Dulan
TOE TAGZ I II III IV
LEVELS TO THIS SHYT I II
IT'S JUST ME AND YOU
By Ah'Million
KINGPIN DREAMS I II III
RAN OFF ON DA PLUG
By Paper Boi Rari
CONFESSIONS OF A GANGSTA I II III IV
CONFESSIONS OF A JACKBOY I II
By Nicholas Lock
I'M NOTHING WITHOUT HIS LOVE
SINS OF A THUG
TO THE THUG I LOVED BEFORE
A GANGSTA SAVED XMAS
IN A HUSTLER I TRUST
By Monet Dragun
CAUGHT UP IN THE LIFE I II III
THE STREETS NEVER LET GO I II III

By Robert Baptiste
NEW TO THE GAME I II III
MONEY, MURDER & MEMORIES I II III
By Malik D. Rice
LIFE OF A SAVAGE I II III IV
A GANGSTA'S QUR'AN I II III IV
MURDA SEASON I II III
GANGLAND CARTEL I II III
CHI'RAQ GANGSTAS I II III IV
KILLERS ON ELM STREET I II III
JACK BOYZ N DA BRONX I II III
A DOPEBOY'S DREAM I II III
JACK BOYS VS DOPE BOYS I II III
COKE GIRLZ
COKE BOYS
SOSA GANG I II
BRONX SAVAGES
BODYMORE KINGPINS
By Romell Tukes
LOYALTY AIN'T PROMISED I II
By Keith Williams
QUIET MONEY I II III
THUG LIFE I II III
EXTENDED CLIP I II
A GANGSTA'S PARADISE
By Trai'Quan
THE STREETS MADE ME I II III
By Larry D. Wright
THE ULTIMATE SACRIFICE I, II, III, IV, V, VI
KHADIFI
IF YOU CROSS ME ONCE I II
ANGEL I II III IV
IN THE BLINK OF AN EYE
By Anthony Fields
THE LIFE OF A HOOD STAR

By Ca$h & Rashia Wilson
THE STREETS WILL NEVER CLOSE I II III
By K'ajji
CREAM I II III
THE STREETS WILL TALK
By Yolanda Moore
NIGHTMARES OF A HUSTLA I II III
By King Dream
CONCRETE KILLA I II III
VICIOUS LOYALTY I II III
By Kingpen
HARD AND RUTHLESS I II
MOB TOWN 251
THE BILLIONAIRE BENTLEYS I II III
REAL G'S MOVE IN SILENCE
By Von Diesel
GHOST MOB
Stilloan Robinson
MOB TIES I II III IV V VI
SOUL OF A HUSTLER, HEART OF A KILLER I II
GORILLAZ IN THE TRENCHES
By SayNoMore
BODYMORE MURDERLAND I II III
THE BIRTH OF A GANGSTER I II
By Delmont Player
FOR THE LOVE OF A BOSS
By C. D. Blue
MOBBED UP I II III IV
THE BRICK MAN I II III IV V
THE COCAINE PRINCESS I II III IV V VI VII
By King Rio
KILLA KOUNTY I II III IV
By Khufu
MONEY GAME I II
By Smoove Dolla

A GANGSTA'S KARMA I II III
By FLAME
KING OF THE TRENCHES I II III
by GHOST & TRANAY ADAMS
QUEEN OF THE ZOO I II
By Black Migo
GRIMEY WAYS I II III
By Ray Vinci
XMAS WITH AN ATL SHOOTER
By Ca$h & Destiny Skai
KING KILLA
By Vincent "Vitto" Holloway
BETRAYAL OF A THUG I II
By Fre$h
THE MURDER QUEENS I II
By Michael Gallon
TREAL LOVE
By Le'Monica Jackson
FOR THE LOVE OF BLOOD I II
By Jamel Mitchell
HOOD CONSIGLIERE I II
By Keese
PROTÉGÉ OF A LEGEND I II
LOVE IN THE TRENCHES
By Corey Robinson
BORN IN THE GRAVE I II III
By Self Made Tay
MOAN IN MY MOUTH
By XTASY
TORN BETWEEN A GANGSTER AND A GENTLEMAN
By J-BLUNT & Miss Kim
LOYALTY IS EVERYTHING I II
Molotti
HERE TODAY GONE TOMORROW
By Fly Rock

PILLOW PRINCESS
By S. Hawkins

BOOKS BY LDP'S CEO, CA$H

TRUST IN NO MAN
TRUST IN NO MAN 2
TRUST IN NO MAN 3
BONDED BY BLOOD
SHORTY GOT A THUG
THUGS CRY
THUGS CRY 2
THUGS CRY 3
TRUST NO BITCH
TRUST NO BITCH 2
TRUST NO BITCH 3
TIL MY CASKET DROPS
RESTRAINING ORDER
RESTRAINING ORDER 2
IN LOVE WITH A CONVICT
LIFE OF A HOOD STAR
XMAS WITH AN ATL SHOOTER